Manx Faeries

The Little People of the Isle of Man

JOHN KRUSE

GREEN MAGIC

Manx Faeries © 2021 by John Kruse. All rights reserved.
No part of this book may be used or reproduced in any form
without written permission of the authors, except in the case
of quotations in articles and reviews.

Green Magic
Seed Factory
Aller
Langport
Somerset
TA10 0QN
England

www.greenmagicpublishing.com

Designed & typeset by K.DESIGN
Winscombe, Somerset

ISBN 9781838418533

GREEN MAGIC

Contents

Introduction	7
Appearance	11
Stature & Physique	11
Clothes	17
Smell	19
Speech	20
Habits & Character	22
Temperament	22
Fairy Times	23
Fairy Gatherings	24
Faery Dwellings	25
Faery Routes	27
Faery Flocks	28
Fairy Games & Dances	30
Washing	31
Elder Trees	32
Faery Hunts	34
Fairy Fleets	35
Fairy Fighting	37
Water Spirits	39
Mermaids	39

Other Marine Spirits	44
Fresh Water Spirits	46
Water Bulls	48
Water Horses	52
Other Water Sprites	55

Manx Bogies and Goblins … 58
Bugganes	58
Fynoderee	64
Glashtyn	69

Faery Beasts … 71
Faery Horses	71
Faery Pig	73
Faery Sheep	74
Faery Cattle	75
Faery Hounds	75
Faery Cats	78

Human Relations … 79
Faery Rules	80
Protections Against Faeries	82
Faeries in Human Homes	88
Faery Thefts	91
Predicting the Future	94
Disrespecting Faeries	96
Changelings	102
Faery Abductions of Children	110
Faery Abductions of Adults	113
Being with the Faeries	117
Faery Mischief	118

    Faery Music … … … … … … … … … … … … … 121
    Faery Gold … … … … … … … … … … … … … 123
    The Lhiannan Shee … … … … … … … … … … 125

Manx Fairies Today … … … … … … … … … … … …**134**

Bibliography … … … … … … … … … … … … …**137**

Appendix: Manx Fairy Poetry … … … … … … … …**139**
    William Harrison, Y Phynnodderee… … … … … … 139
    Cushag: Margaret Letitia Josephine Kermode … … … 144
    Guillyn Veggey: "The Lil Fallas" … … … … … … … 145
    The Phynodderee… … … … … … … … … … … 146
    The Passing of The Fayries … … … … … … … … 148
    The Ride… … … … … … … … … … … … … … 150
    (from) The Babe of Earey Cushlin … … … … … … 153
    The Wans From Up … … … … … … … … … … 158

Introduction

The Isle of Man is full of faery beings. In a concentrated area, it has all the most fascinating supernatural creatures of the British Isles, not just fairies, but various goblins, faery beasts and mermaids. It provides a fascinating case study of the wider wonders of British faery-lore, a kind of microcosm of Britain's faeries.

The island's fairies go by a variety of euphemisms, being referred to as the little folk or little people, the crowd, the mob, themselves.[1] They are often termed, more directly, the *ferrish* (singular)/*ferrishyn* (plural). This *could* be a Manx word, but if we compare authentically Manx Celtic phrases like *mooinjer veggy* or *sleigh beggey*, both of which mean the little people (or 'host' – compare the Scottish Gaelic *sluagh*), and *guillyn veggey* (little boys), we may see that it's probably not a native Manx term. *Ferrishyn* seems suspiciously similar, to me, to the words *ferishers*, *feriers*, *fraries* and, even, *farisees*/ *pharisees* used in Norfolk and Suffolk in the east of England. On Orkney and Shetland, you might also encounter the pronunciation *ferries*. Recalling the Highland Gaelic tendency to turn a final 's' into 'sh', this could very well indicate the route by which Manx speakers arrived at *ferrish*. Whatever the exact derivation, these are all dialect versions of the English 'fairies' and, as such, aren't themselves hugely old. The word *feorin*, used in the English North West, would appear to be the nearest possible source, but it is most probably derived from 'fear' – something that scares you.

---

1 Gill, *Second Manx Scrapbook*, c.6.

"Fairies can be found practically anywhere in the island" declared the folklore writer calling herself 'Mona Douglas.' She then proceeded to offer a unique taxonomy of the Manx fairies that appears to draw on Irish mythology and which doesn't seem to be entirely supported by the faerylore of the island. She distinguished the *guillyn beggey*, 'the little fellows' who are the size of children, the *cloan moyrney*, the 'proud clan,' who are tall and beautiful, and the *sleih shee* or 'people of peace,' who are of more ethereal countenance. These euphemisms were unquestionably applied to the faery folk to avoid naming them directly, but it is not certain that they reflected strict divisions in type – as we shall see.[2]

On the Isle of Man, the prevailing belief was that the fairies represented the souls of those who died long ago, possibly before the Biblical flood, or were perhaps amongst the angels banished from heaven – hence the protective prayer "*jee saue mee voish cloan ny moyrn*" ('God save me from the children of pride').[3] The spiritual nature of the 'Little People' was accepted by those Manx informants who supplied information for Walter Evans Wentz' *Fairy Faith in the Celtic Countries* of 1911. As ghosts or spirits of the dead, one witness termed the fairies 'Middle World Men,' who weren't good enough for heaven or bad enough for hell, but lived in a world of their own. In light of this, it is interesting to note that, near Cronk ny Irree Laa, on the Dalby Mountain, there is a spot where you can place your ear on the ground and hear what are called 'the sounds of infinity' (*sheean ny feaynid*). It is said that these are the sounds of the invisible beings who fill space – trapped, as it were, between the earth and heaven. Another of Evans Wentz' witnesses explained that some of the fairies were evil spirits, immortal and insubstantial – "like shadows on the wall." The precise distinctions

---

2   Mona Douglas, 'Secret Land of Legends,' *The Times*, Jan.2nd 1970, 27.
3   Evans Wentz, *Fairy Faith*, 121, 123, 124, 125 & 129; Gill, *Third Manx Scrapbook*, Part 2, c.3.

made between many supernatural forms are, nonetheless, far from clear: as folklorist Walter Gill observed, "The fairies again are not always clearly distinguishable from guardian spirits, or from evil spirits which have never been humanly embodied, or from the spirits of the dead. Nor are intelligent spirits fully differentiated from the automatic phenomena more commonly termed ghosts."[4]

Another of the Manx witnesses interviewed by Evans Wentz, John Davies of Ballasalla, told him that "There are as many kinds of fairies as populations in our world." Walter Gill confirmed a few years later in 1913 that fairies of all sizes and descriptions live on Man. They seem to have filled every corner of the island – with the consequence, as another writer observed, that superstitious fear of them used to keep the peasants safely inside their homes at night. The fact of their omnipresence is attested by the sheer number of fairy placenames – wells, hills, bridges and such like – that are to be found across the Isle of Man. Sophia Morrison, in the preface to the chapter on Manx fairies in Walter Evans Wentz' book, wrote that the "Manx hierarchy of fairy beings peoples hills and glens, caves and rivers, mounds and roads [and] their name is legion."[5]

Although no previous commentators have suggested it, I think it's worth noting the theory that the Manx fairies may well be regarded as 'spirits of place,' *genii loci* of the island landscape. Many beings are associated with particular wells, pools and hills; the hob-like *fynoderee* is said to bring prosperity and fertility to the farm it works upon; overall, the robust and sometimes violent temperament of the Manx *ferrishyn* could well be regarded as a manifestation of the sometimes harsh and rugged nature of the terrain within which

---

[4] Evans Wentz, 117, 120, 124, 125 & 130; S. Morrison, 'Manx Dialect Connected with Fairies,' *Proceedings of the Isle of Man Natural History & Archaeological Society*, vol.1 (New Series), 1906; Gill, *Second Manx Scrapbook*, c.2.
[5] *Fairy Faith*, 123; *Mannin*, no.2, 1913; Cumming, *Isle of Man*, 29; Gill, *Second Manx Scrapbook*, c.6.

they live. The Manx faeries cannot be separated from the island on which they developed; they are an integral part of its landscape and climate.

The variety of faery beings on Man is, indeed, remarkable – including not just the conventional humanoid fairies but supernatural dogs and pigs, water-dwelling bulls and horses, marine and riverine spirits, hairy goblins and shapeshifting monsters, such as the buggane.

The faery lore of the Isle of Man is rich, surprising and complex. We also have the great good fortune that it has been studied and recorded for nearly three hundred years. The first detailed account was given by English civil servant George Waldron in 1731; then, in late Victorian and Edwardian times, a considerable number of folklorists, including such distinguished figures as Professor John Rhys, Charles Roeder (Karl Röder) and Walter Gill, made dedicated efforts to collect as much information as they could. For a relatively small island, we have a wealth of resources to draw upon and, as a result, we are able to provide a comprehensive statement of all aspects of Manx faery life.

Appearance

John Davies, a herb doctor and seer of Ballasalla, remarked in 1910 on the variety of types of fairy on the Isle of Man, illustrating this by saying that "I have seen some who were about two and a half feet high and some who were as big as we are." There is as much difference between fairies as there is between human peoples. What exactly *do* they look like, then?[6]

Stature & Physique

'*Yn mooinjer veggey*,' the little people, as they're called, plainly got their name for a reason. What can be said about the physical appearance of the Manx fairies? The sightings describe a range in sizes, from tiny up to the height of a child of seven or eight. Interestingly, too, the Manx are said not to be as small as English fairies are – or at least, have come to be perceived.[7]

Scottish faery-lore expert John Francis Campbell claimed in 1862 that Manx fairies have neither bodes nor bones. They are partly human and partly spiritual in their nature, he said, and are visible to men only when they choose. It's not clear what Campbell's source was for this statement; most Manx witnesses don't seem to doubt the corporeality of the faeries they have seen, although they do often acknowledge that they may be less robust or solid than us. For

---

6   Wentz 123.
7   Robertson, *A Tour,* 76; Mona Douglas, 'Secret Land of Legends,' *The Times,* Jan.2nd 1970, 27.

instance, one writer described them as small and delicate, looking handsome from a distance but up close be revealed as decrepit and withered. Another witness felt them walk on her and said they were "as light as cats." A further witness confirmed that they were "very little and very light," yet again, a certain Mr Collister saw them once playing in the parlour of his house and described then as "lumps of boys," which implies that, whilst they may not have been very tall, they were solid enough.[8]

Many accounts agree that the *ferrishyn* are indeed small. A man who lived on the Howe in Rushen was crossing a field called the Naiee Veg late one night, and he saw a flock of little white things jumping about by his side. At first, he thought they were ponies, albeit very small ones; then they suddenly changed into tiny women and flew at him. He took to his heels and they pursued him. They were gaining on him and he feared being caught, but he just managed to get home and slam the door in their faces. The terror instilled by these tiny beings was so great that, the next morning, he was unable to stand and lost the use of his legs for several months.[9]

One fairy sighted in the road by two boys was five to six inches tall, had a pale face with no beard, tiny feet and shoes, tiny ears that they compared to shirt buttons and was dressed in blue. They tried to catch him but he spread his coat flaps and flew high up into the sky, leaving no footprints behind in the dust.[10]

Thomas Radcliffe and a friend from Sulby village were walking home late one night from Ballalaigh when they saw twelve to fourteen little people run across the road just ahead of them. Despite their height, the pair didn't think these beings were children as it was so late and because they could find no trace of them where they'd

---

[8] Campbell, *Popular Tales of the West Highlands*, vol.1, 81, A. Moore, *Folklore of the Isle of Man*, c.3; *Yn Lioar Manninagh*, III; Roeder, *Manx Folktales*, 11.
[9] Gill, *Third Manx Scrapbook*, Part 2, c.3.
[10] *Manx Notes & Queries*, 1904, 117.

APPEARANCE

just crossed the highway. The men concluded they must have been fairies. Similarly, in 1888 a man called John Radcliffe was shooting at Lezayre Wood when he saw two little figures peeking at him from behind a tree. At first, he thought they must be the children of the woodsman but they were very small and clothed in brown, so he concluded they had to be fairies. Crowds of fairies seen near Ballasalla were also described as being "like little boys." Some other fairies, spotted walking along the top of a wall at Ballaugh, were estimated to have been about two feet high. Dora Broome described the *mooinjer veggey* as being "just the height of a man's elbow."[11]

Not infrequently, although the fairies are as tall as infants, other features prevent them being mistaken for children. In 1912 at Ramsey, for instance, a little old man was sighted, wearing a red cap and blue coat. He had white hair and a beard and very bright blue eyes and was carrying a lantern. A very similar small man sat on the chest of a quarry worker taking at lunchtime nap at the Glen Auldyn quarries, only a short distance away from Ramsey. Once, two children were approached by two fairies, whom they described as being "withered hobgoblins, three feet high, clad in little jackets and shorty red petticoats." These fairies were advancing hand in hand, as if to speak to the children, but they didn't hang around to find out more.[12]

Not all of the Manx fairies seem to be small, though; some look like adults to us rather than children. At Peel Castle "big fairies" used to be seen, sometimes climbing up and down the flagpoles. They would also be sighted on the ramparts and, if they were there shouting with men's voices when the fishing boats were putting out to sea, this would be taken as a sign of imminent bad weather and the boats would sail back to the quay. An Edwardian witness, a Mr J. H. Kelly, described how he had once met "four figures as real

---

[11] *Yn Lioar Manninagh*, 3, 182; Wentz 125; Gill, *Second Manx Scrapbook*, c.6; Broome, *More Fairy Tales*, 10.
[12] Gill, *Second Manx Scrapbook*, c.6; *Chambers Journal*, vol.24, 1855, 96.

to look upon as human beings, and of medium size, though I am certain they were not human." We should bear in mind, though, that these differences in size need not indicate different types of fairies. The fairies wield magical powers and they can appear to us to be small – but they can just as easily make themselves big, if and when they want to.[13]

The fairies can also melt away using their glamour. An Arbory man and his sister once found the road ahead of them blocked by a great crowd of people so dense that they could not see through. As they got nearer to the throng, though, it simply vanished. It seems very likely that this magical ability to shrink and swell, appear and disappear, may have contributed to the idea that the Manx fairies had no physical body.[14]

Nowadays, we tend to expect fairies to resemble us quite closely, but they can be much stranger than that. For example, some fairy beings seen in a slate quarry at Glen Auldyn were described as being twelve to eighteen inches high, with bodies that were grey like fungus, swollen in front but overall resembling tiny men. They were holding hands and dancing in a circle.[15]

Besides their stature, there are very often other distinguishing and unusual features to the fairies. Some were seen that had oversized ears that looked like wine (or Dutch gin) bottles, others have feathers growing amongst their hair. As a rule, though, the fairies have red hair and (it is reported) prefer red headed humans.[16]

Faery eyes are noted in particular for being distinctive: they may be very brilliant, oddly shaped or oddly coloured. One witness described their eyes as being very small. Some faeries once seen on

---

13 Gill, *Manx Scrapbook*, c.4 'German;' Wentz 134; Roeder, *Manx Folktales*, 3; Broome, *Fairy Tales*, 106.
14 Wentz 126.
15 Gill, *Second Manx Scrapbook*, c.6.
16 Gill, *Second Manx Scrapbook*, c.6.

the island were said to look like pretty little girls – except that they had scaly, fish-like hands.[17]

This last detail also reminds us that it is our habit, currently, to assume that fairies will look like attractive females. This assumption is demonstrated by a statement that Manx fairy women are generally very happy and beautiful, although they usually vanish as soon as you catch a glimpse of them. May that as it may, other accounts already cited remind us that we should not assume that the *ferrishyn* will always be good looking; in fact, there can be aspects to the faery appearance that are frankly terrifying. Pity the boy who woke up one night hungry and decided to sneak into the kitchen to steal a freshly baked 'bonnag' (bannock). Sitting before the fire, warming his hands, was a hideous fairy man with claw like hands and staring red eyes; the child ran swiftly back to bed, still hungry.[18]

The evidence goes further still, however, and fairies are encountered that are not human-like at all. For instance, a man from Arbory parish once saw fairies in the form of a herd of little black pigs, filling the road. He asked them who, in the name of god, they were and they immediately disappeared. A second witness, from Agneish, was once met on Slieu Reay hill by something that resembled a snowy white unicorn. The man blessed himself and it vanished.[19]

Even if the figure is partly human, there can be something strange about it. In 1922 a woman was cycling from Peel to Dalby one evening. She happened to look over her shoulder and saw in the distance what looked like a horse, but with a man's head and face, the whole apparition being pale grey or white in colour. This alarming creature was following her and, what's more, was gaining on her. She pedalled hard up the hill in a panic, expecting soon to

---

17   Gill, *Third Manx Scrapbook*, Part 2, c.3; *Yn Lioar Manninagh*, III.
18   Robertson, *A Tour*, 76; Roeder, *Manx Folktales*, 16.
19   Wentz 126; Jenkinson, *Practical Guide*, 106.

hear the sound of galloping hoofs, but the being had vanished. In the Patrick parish, at Droghad Ruy, the road crosses the river at a spot called the Fairy Glen. A woman was gathering blackberries there one afternoon in about 1920 when a sudden mist descended and she saw a shape like a man running down the upper part of the ravine towards the road. He "looked as if he was coming loose, all falling to pieces" she recalled and, feeling that there was something uncanny going on, she hurried away with her half-filled basket of berries to shelter at the nearest house.[20]

There are manifestations weirder even than these, in fact. In two examples, bugganes took on the form of bizarre rolling, burning wheels:

> "A man, when he was young, was seeing the girls home late in the night, and when coming to the end of *beyr yn clagh glass* (the grey stone road), he heard a great noise, and he looked in every direction, but could see nothing, and the noise was coming nearer. He did not know what to do, so he got over the hedge, but the noise was just over him, and he looked up and saw a thing like a big wheel of fire. It was going round at a great speed, and went towards Ballacurry and when it was near that place it vanished, and he saw no more of it.
>
> *Second Account* – A man was coming along the grey stone road in *Ballakillowey* and he met a big wheel of fire, going around at a fearful rate, but remaining in the same place, and he could not get past, so he went back and took another road, but he met the wheel again at the next opening, and he went across the fields to shun it, but when he came to the high road the wheel was there again, but he ventured to pass it and got away. It made a great noise with whirling round."[21]

---

20 Gill, *Manx Scrapbook*, c.4, 'Patrick' & *Second Manx Scrapbook*, c.6(3).
21 *Manx Notes and Queries*, 1904, 186.

APPEARANCE

Another incident, reported in 1852, is very similar. A man out walking saw a seated person whom he took to be a soldier from the Castletown barracks. The walker had recently heard the evening bugle sound and approached the soldier to tell him this. The figure vanished into the air, though, and a ball of fire then proceeded before the first man all the way to his home.[22]

All three of these apparitions seemed to be alight. In another sighting, the fairies seemed to give off some sort of aura. A man was walking one October night when he saw the fairies assembled across a river within a "a circle of supernatural light," what he called an "astral light" or 'the light of Nature.' In fact, the Manx fairies can appear without having any tangible, physical form at all. Walter Gill recorded in his *Second Manx Scrapbook* of 1932 that they might be seen far off at night as sparks or little flames dancing on the hilltops.[23]

These last examples may strain our preconceived categories as to what a 'faery' is, but these Manx examples are far from unique. A number of very similar experiences have been described by Scottish witnesses, forcing us to acknowledge that the supernatural world is far stranger and more alarming than images of Tinker Bell and the Little Mermaid might lead us to assume.[24]

Clothes

One of Walter Evans Wentz' witnesses told him that the fairies were the spirits of the dead and that, as such, they appeared to him, "in the same dress as in the days when they lived here on earth." What *do* our sources tell us about fairy clothing?[25]

---

22 *Yn Lioar Manninagh*, vol.1, part 2, 290.
23 Evans-Wentz, 133; Gill, *Second Manx Scrapbook*, c.6.
24 See my *Beyond Faery*, 2020, c.9.
25 Wentz 123.

Certainly, at Claghyn Baney in Patrick parish, a group of children playing in a ruined cottage in the mid-1920s saw some fairies climbing in and out of the windows; they were "little men in tail-coats and little hats" which seemed to be of the cocked or three-cornered variety. In another case a 'fairy bishop' visited a woman living at South Barrule who was sick in bed. He too wore a tricorn hat of the eighteenth-century fashion – and shared an oatcake with her.[26]

Normally, though, it appears to be the colouring of the fairies' clothing that is distinctive, rather than its style. Some faeries seen at East Baldwin in the early nineteenth century were reported to be like small dogs running about – except that they wore red caps. The witness said he had not been afraid; he knew that as long as the fairies were not disturbed, they would not harm him. In another case, a man reported encountering a number of "little fellows," about two to three feet in height and wearing red caps, who all ran way when they saw the human.[27]

Fairies seen at Slieu Reay were said to be little beings in red trousers and blue coats. Another writer confirmed that little folk are usually dressed in blue or green, with peaked caps of red material, which are regularly said to be made of leather. Sometimes the caps are said to be adorned with fairy lace.[28]

Female Manx fairies are very often described as 'little red women,' reflecting their short stature and red cloaks. For example, a man who sat down to rest as he walked home one night along the coast from Laxey to Maughold. He fell asleep briefly and was amazed when he awoke to find a little fairy woman in red, sitting in his lap.[29]

---

26 Gill, *Manx Scrapbook*, c.4, 'Patrick;' Roeder, *Manx Folklore*, 11.
27 Jenkinson, *Practical Guide to the Isle of Man*, 39; Gill, *Second Manx Scrapbook*, c.6.
28 Jenkinson, *Practical Guide*, 106; Moore, *Folklore of the Isle of Man*, c.3; *Yn Lioar Manninagh*, III; S. Morrison, 'Manx Dialect Connected with Fairies,' *Proceedings of the Isle of Man Natural History & Archaeological Society*, vol.1 (New Series), 1906.
29 Gill, *Third Manx Scrapbook*, Part 2, c.3.

APPEARANCE

In much of Britain, green is regarded as the distinctively fairy colour, and it is certainly not absent from Manx reports, though far less popular than red. Perhaps the season has an influence on clothing choice, for the fairies have been seen on summer evenings, dressed all in green. Another writer described them as being dressed in green with red caps – and with very small eyes.[30]

Smell

On the island, the upper parts of glens on the isle are reputed to be the best places to see, hear *and to smell* the faeries where the fairies have been during the night. What you will encounter is a peculiar, lingering sour odour, apparently, akin to the smell of a deep gill on a summer's day.[31]

That the fairies seem to have a distinguishing scent is confirmed in several reports. For instance, a certain Mrs C., living in Arbory parish, one day in December 1891 went to the stream near her cottage to collect water. There was, she said, a terrible stench "between a burnt rag and a stink," and so "thick" on the bank that she could scarcely breathe. This was the smell of fairies, who had obviously only recently departed. A girl on the island also smelled them once – and then lost her sense of smell – although this could conceivably have been a punishment for her involuntary exclamation of "What a stink!" which would naturally have offended the sensitive little people (her sister, who was with her, sensibly kept quiet and was unharmed).[32]

It's fair to remark, though, that the fairies themselves object to nasty, evil smells – such as stale urine (*mooin*). We should not assume, either, that we are ourselves either odourless or perfumed.

---

30 Train, *Isle of Man*, vol.2, c.XVIII; Roeder, *Manx Folktales*, 11.
31 *Yn Lioar Manninagh*, vol.4. 161.
32 *Yn Lioar Manninagh*, vol.2, 194–7.

In one story a man was walking from Peel to Surby across the mountains when he came across a fine house. He was offered lodging for the night but had to be hidden when *ferrishyn* visitors arrived. His concealment notwithstanding, his presence inside a barrel was easily exposed by their sensitive noses. As soon as he'd been found, the house and all the company evaporated, leaving the man sitting alone on the moor in the sunshine. Secondly, a very grubby fisherman from Port Erin was forcibly washed by the fairies. Whilst it's true that he'd seen them swinging on the gorse, dressed in their red caps and red and green clothes, this punishment was evidently about something more than his intrusion on their privacy.[33]

Speech

Sometimes, you neither see (nor smell) the fairies, but only hear their voices, which have a reputation for being very loud. For example, they may be heard shouting – and their children crying – in the East Baldwin Hills, and this has even been loud enough to be heard from ships offshore. A puzzling story from Port Erin, that seems to be related to this, recounts how a fishing party out at sea heard cries of distress coming from Cronk ny Irey Lhaa mountain. Another vessel, sailing nearer to shore, heard the same calls and, one night, one of the crew shouted in reply "If you're a boy, I name you John; if you're girl, Judith." The fairy cries ceased and were never heard again.[34]

It appears that, a lot of the time at least, the Manx fairies spoke Manx, what the native islanders called *Gaelg*. A few recorded accounts confirm that the fairies were to be heard conversing in '*yallick*.' This seems to have been taken rather for granted (as they

---

33   *Yn Lioar Manninagh,* vol.III; Herbert, *The Isle of Man,* 173.
34   Jenkinson, *Practical Guide,* 40; W. Martin, 'Collectanea – Goblins in the Isle of Man,' *Folklore,* vol.13, 1902, 186; see too *Manx Notes & Queries,* 1904, 129 & 130.

are the original inhabitants of the island), but all the same there are other reports in which they are said to speak "a foreign tongue." They may often be overheard talking together at night, but they cannot be understood. In fact, the incomprehensibility of faery speech is repeatedly stressed by witnesses.[35]

Manx folklore expert Charles Roeder, in his book *Skeealyn Cheeil Chiolee* (Manx Folk Tales), reported the following local theory about their speech:

> "I have not heard anything about the fairies this long time. There is no-one hearing them but the woman in the little shop. She heard them at midnight one winter night in an elder tree, speaking a language she couldn't understand. As she drew near, they whispered in her ear – but she couldn't understand. Perhaps they were foreign fairies, visiting the Isle of Man, for in old tales the fairies speak Manx. The Manx fairies have gone, or they have changed their language – like the people. Perhaps the fairies couldn't understand English so they changed their language out of spite: they can be spiteful when offended."

Another witness suggested to Roeder that "perhaps this [unknown] language is the language of fairyland, but whether that's above or below earth no-one can tell."[36]

---

35 See for example, *Manx Notes & Queries*, 1904, 118 & 129; *Yn Lioar Manninagh*, vol. III.
36 Roeder, *Manx Folktales*, 1–2.

Habits & Character

In 1910, a Mr T. Kermode, of the Lower House of the Manx Parliament, expressed the view that "the fairies [are] a complete nation or world in themselves, distinct from our world, but having habits and instincts like ours. Social organisation among them is said to be similar to that among men, and they have their soldiers and commanders." How, in fact, is Manx Faery organised and what are its inhabitants' habits and manners?[37]

Temperament

A visitor to Man in 1794 was told by an elderly inhabitant that "notwithstanding all the holy sprinklings of the priests in former days, the fairies still haunted many places in the island" and that there were two broad tribes: the "playful, benignant spirits, and those who were sullen and vindictive." This informant claimed often to have seen the former on fine summer evenings, sitting by brooks and waterfalls, half concealed amongst bushes, or dancing on mountain tops. They were happy, beautiful and small in stature (but not tiny). They were shy, as well, and would disappear at the

---

37   Wentz 134.

merest glance from a human. "These sportive beings rejoiced in the happiness of mortals, but the sullen fairies delighted in procuring human misery." The latter group lived apart from the others and were neither good-looking nor well-dressed. They were generally enveloped in cloud or mountain fog or they haunted caves in cliffs. They brought storms and waves along the coast.[38]

Despite this individual's division of the little folk into 'good' and 'bad,' the evidence set out in the rest of this book will indicate that the 'bad' fairies are much more likely to be encountered upon Man than the good – or, perhaps, it would be better to say that the normal disposition of the Manx faeries was antagonistic. Unquestionably, as we shall see, the *ferrishyn* are vindictive if annoyed and can be spiteful and cruel if they're made angry.[39]

Fairy Times

There are certain hours and seasons when you are more likely to meet the fairies on the island. They are generally abroad at night and they especially come out at harvest moon (*rehollys vooar yn aiyr*).[40] They are also out in the world and more dangerous than usual on May Eve (*Laa Boaldyn*) and Halloween, when people will take special measures to protect themselves and their livestock.[41]

Manx antiquary William Harrison recorded the popular belief (not only on Man but across the British Isles) that it was on Hollantide Eve (November 11th, called *Hop-tu-naa* on Man) that the 'hogmen' or 'hillmen,' the fairies living in the mounds, moved to new dwellings and that a general fairy 'flitting' took place. Inevitably, at such time a time the Little Folk were to be met with

---

38 D. Robertson, *A Tour Through the Isle of Man*, 1794, 75–6.
39 Roeder, *Manx Folktales*, 3.
40 Train, *Isle of Man*, vol.2, c.XVIII.
41 Leney, *Shadowland in Ellan Vannin*, 144 & 146.

in all directions, hence the wish to propitiate and protect against them. Harrison quoted from an old Manx rhyme recited on the occasion – "*Hop-tu-naa* – this is old Hollantide night;/ *Trolla-laa* – the moon shines fair and bright," explaining that *trolla-laa* was a slightly mangled form of a Norse phrase, *trolle á lae*, (trolls/ elves into the sea). The use of 'troll' is very likely to be an echo of Man's Viking past and might well indicate too that the first element of 'hogmen' is the Old Norse word *haugr* or *høg*, meaning a mound or hillock. [42]

Fairy Gatherings

Fires and unexplained lights frequently mark the fact that the fairies are out and about and enjoying themselves. For instance, mysterious lights have often been seen on cliffs and headlands, travelling along a highway or in empty or derelict houses.[43]

A man once saw a bonfire at Glenchass, near Fistard, but there was no sign of any fire at the spot in the morning; again, numerous times the same individual had seen Perwick Brows on fire at the night, but there was never any trace of burning there the next day. These nocturnal illuminations are often associated with the sound of fairy voices mentioned at the end of the last chapter. For example, some men were going home from Port St. Mary about one o'clock on Saturday night, and saw a large fire coming in from sea. At the same time, they heard the sound of drunken voices quarrelling and fighting coming from the place called Four Roads. The fire travelled towards the place and disappeared there, at which point the arguments ceased as well.[44]

---

42 W. Harrison, *A Mona Miscellany*, Manx Society vol.16, 1869, 148.
43 *Manx Notes & Queries*, 1904, 143; Gill, *Third Manx Scrapbook*, Part 2, c.3, section 6.
44 *Manx Notes & Queries*, 1904, 129 & 130.

Another man was travelling to Cregneash late one night and, when he reached Crosh Molley Mooar, he heard great laughing and sport ahead at Poyll Vill and, as he got nearer, he saw what appeared to be a great crowd of gentlemen and ladies dancing in rings, others playing ' kiss in the ring,' and others jumping, all of whom were dressed in great finery. He stood for some time watching them, and they kept on dancing, jumping, laughing, and shouting away and did not seem to take any notice of the human spectator. Another local man was on his way home from Port Erin, and also met with a great crowd at Crosh Molley. However, this time, they were aware of the human presence and the man was seized and was obliged to go with them. When they got to Poyll Vill they met a very big being, who criticised the crowd of fairies for forcing the human to go with them. "Let the decent man go" he said, "right before the wind." The man was released and found himself blown home as fast he could travel. Many other people have reported seeing large fairy crowds at Crosh Molley but, when they got near, the throngs had vanished.[45]

Faery Dwellings

The fairies live in mounds, tumuli or in hollow hills; some are found living under human houses and other buildings.[46] There is said to be a fairy hill at Rushen where feasts and dances are held and others are identified in the Fairy Saddle at Ballafletcher and at Cronk Mooar, the Neolithic barrow outside Bradda, where fairy funerals are often seen. The latter site is said, too, to be the hall of the fairy king (*ray shee*). If indeed there are fairy royalty on Man, we hear little about them otherwise from the folklore, although one source states that the king is called (prosaically) Philip and his queen is named Bahee,

---

45   *Manx Notes & Queries*, 1904, 189.
46   Campbell, *Popular Tales of the West Highlands*, vol.1, 81; *Manx Notes & Queries*, 1904, 116; Broome, *Fairy Tales*, 66 & 95.

which is at least exotic enough to sound more authentic. If there are monarchs, they may well live in the 'fairy palace' that was seen in Glen Helen. Music was issuing from the structure, which was described as being like a "great glass house... all lit up."[47]

The *ferrishyn* have a 'city' at Skyhill, above Ramsey, apparently. A man crossing the hill here one night was taken by them and found himself inside a large hall at a feast. None of the fairies spotted he was there, so he kept quiet in the shadows and watched the celebration. He fell asleep where he was concealed and awoke the next morning, lying on a bed of fern on the top of Skyhill.[48]

As well as their own homes, the Manx faeries had a persistent liking for human buildings. At Lonan, there was an example of what was called a 'Fairy House' (*Thie Ferrishyn*) which was the first or oldest dwelling in a village. The local fairies would be fondest of this and would spend more time there than in any other residence in the place. Fairy music and other noises were sometimes heard coming from the Lonan cottage. Such cases of peaceful co-existence are, however, rare, as we shall see later.[49]

The *ferrishyn* are also widely known to use mills at night. For instance, when the mill at Kiondroghad on the Isle of Man was run overnight one time, the local faeries threw a broom at the millers in warning. They may have disliked the noise – but they might just as well have been objecting to what they regarded as an intrusion upon their rightful evening use of the mill. It is frequently said that the faeries hate human noise and they're said to have particular objections the ringing of church bells, but this may be just as much a matter of the associations as the sound itself. Even so, another witness reported that at Keeil Moray, near Glen Maye, a little fairy

---

[47] Train, *Isle of Man*, vol.2, c.XVIII; Jenkinson, *Practical Guide*, 36; Gill, *Second Man Scrapbook*, c.6; Wentz 131.
[48] Gill, *Second Manx Scrapbook*, c.6.
[49] Gill, *Second Manx Scrapbook*, 95-6.

woman in a red cloak was regularly seen heading towards the church, ringing a hand-bell, at the time when the church services began. Perhaps she shared the islanders' faith – but she might have been imitating the humans or perhaps just liked the sound. On the whole, as we'll see, there's a faery antipathy to religion. This belief notwithstanding, it's also said that the fairies will never harm an individual on an errand of mercy or charity.[50]

Faery Routes

The Manx faes seemingly enjoy processing in considerable numbers: one time a "small army" of them was sighted; on another occasion, a man came across between one and two thousand faeries who looked like small girls, all of them singing.[51]

The faeries' palaces and hills are connected by 'fairy tracks,' which are said to be guarded by bugganes. The little folk have their regular paths, too, that run between their homes and their favoured meeting places at natural features – pools, trees and meadows.[52]

There can be trouble for the person who gets in the faeries' way when they are on the move. On one such path, there was a gate where a fairy was sometimes seen standing – he looked like a man in a long brown coat with bright buttons, but the figure was of more than human height. Horses disliked passing through the gate late at night, and cattle kept away from it. Each of the two cairns in a field further along the same path was believed to have a guardian buggane. From the ditch alongside a track not far from the gateway a shape resembling a woman used to rise with startling suddenness and follow passers-by, terrifying them with a sound of jingling,

---

50 Gill, *Second Manx Scrapbook*, c.3; *Yn Lioar Manninagh*, vol.3, 155; *Manx Notes & Queries*, 1904, 116; Broome, *More Fairy Tales*, 27; Wentz 118; Cashen, c.2.
51 *Yn Lioar Manninagh*, vol.III.
52 Gill, *Second Manx Scrapbook*, c.6.

clattering and rattling, as if she was covered with chains and cans. The third time that this happened to one man, he stood still and declared "In the name of the Father, and of the Son, and of the Holy Ghost, let this creature be taken away from me! " At that she turned and went back along the field-path to where she had emerged – and was never seen again.[53]

Overall, there seems to be an extremely close link between the Manx fairies and the ancient sites on the island. The last incidents took place very near to two cairns; the fairy gatherings at Crosh Molley Mooar discussed earlier occurred close to the stone circle at Meayll Hill and, as was described, many fairy hills seem to be ancient burial mounds. Given these close associations, it is not surprising to hear that when, in 1859, some archaeologists opened up a barrow near Tynwald Hill, a local farmer sacrificed and burned a heifer there after they had departed, with the aim of atoning to the *ferrishyn* for the desecration of the site. Connected to this seems to be the observation of folklore expert Walter Gill that standing stones at Germans and Michael that are called 'white ladies' (like the spirits that haunt wells) and which were white washed to emphasise their ghostly significance.[54]

Faery Flocks

Whilst the existence of routes between important sites very much implies processions on foot or horseback by the fairies, Manx folklore frequently associates them with movement more akin to that of clouds or flocks of birds or insects.

One particularly vivid description tells how, one moonlit night, a man saw the fairies moving on a hill. There were scores of them, he

---

53 Gill, *Second Manx Scrapbook,* c.6.
54 *Manchester Times,* April 2nd 1881, 4 'Origin of Fairy Superstition;' Gill, *Second Manx Scrapbook,* c.6, section 2.

said, like a black rain cloud. He tried to follow, but they always stayed about twenty or thirty yards ahead of him and they steadily shrank in size until they disappeared completely. It was subsequently found that a girl at a local farm went missing at the same time.[55]

A very similar account concerns a changeling. Its identity was revealed and the human family started building up the fire in order to drive the fairy off (see later). The 'baby' fled when he realised what was happening and the human mother then saw "a flock of low-lying clouds shaped like gulls chasing each other away up Glen Rushen," along with whistles and wicked laughter.[56]

At Cronk Fedjag, in Patrick parish, a man digging turf happened to look up from his work and saw in the distance a great grey cloud moving swiftly towards him. As it came near it solidified into the shape of a hag (caillagh) with teeth as long as his forearm. "What in God's name is this?" he cried out and, at the holy name, the hag melted back into the form of a cloud. She is known as the 'White Lady of the Cronk,' and belongs to the neighbouring hill, Cronk ny Irree Lhaa.[57]

As well as clouds, a fairy host on Man has been described as sounding first like a swarm of humming bees, then like a waterfall and lastly like a marching and murmuring crowd which drew progressively nearer to the witness. Manx folklorist Dora Broome twice described fairies as being "like a swarm of bees" and, in fact, another traditional belief was that 'bumbees' were actually misbehaving fairies who had been turned into insects as a punishment by others in their community.[58]

---

55   *Mannin*, no.2, 1913.
56   Morrison, 'A Manx Changeling Story,' *Folklore*, vol.21, 1910, 472; Morrison, *Manx Fairy Tales*, 85.
57   Gill, *Manx Scrapbook*, c.4, 'Patrick.'
58   Sophia Morrison, *Manx Fairy Tales*, 'Billy Beg, Tom Beg & the Fairies;' Broome, *Fairy Tales*, 67 and *More Fairy Tales* 40; *Notes & Queries*, vol.10, 1854, 500.

Fairy Games & Dances

If you are going to see fairies on Man, you are most likely to see them engaged in some leisure activity, whether that is feasting, dancing or playing some sort of game. The eighteenth-century writer George Waldron described an encounter in which a man saw some boys playing in a field at about three or four o'clock in the afternoon when they should have been at school. He went to tell them off for playing truant but they disappeared as he approached them across the completely open field, making him realise that they hadn't been children at all.[59]

The fairies particularly enjoy dancing to sound of the fiddle; according to one story, their fiddler is a *glashtyn* named Hom Mooar ('big Tom'), whose playing is said to lure humans to enter his hill dancing – and never to return. The sight of fairies dancing seems to have been very common – if not commonplace – at one time. For instance, George Gelling, a joiner at Ballasalla, described in 1910 how his apprentice had once been scared when he looked over a hedge and saw a crowd of little people kicking and dancing. He ran back to the workshop in fright, but the carpenter casually "told him they were nothing but fairies."[60]

Rings mark where the faeries have danced and are commonly seen around the island both on grass and in the snow; flowers shouldn't be picked from such spots or you may be pinched in revenge. The story is also told of an English farmer who bought land near Fairy Bridge during the 1930s and decided to plough up a field containing a fairy ring so that he could plant corn. The night before his first wheat was due to be harvested, a disturbance was heard in the field and, by the light of the new day, it was seen that

---

59   Waldron, *Isle of Man*, 33.
60   Wentz 124.

the entire crop had been flattened, with a perfect, level circle right in the middle.[61]

The whirling movement of the faeries' circle dances even seems to be part of their general nature or motion. In Victorian times, for instance, two men were out walking one night when they saw the figure of a woman dressed all in white standing in the angle of a wall just opposite a church gate. When one of the two men went to speak to her, she took him by the arm and spun him round and round till he was dizzy, and then let go of him so suddenly that he nearly fell down on the road. The marks of her fingers remained on his arm up to the day of his death as dark imprints on the biceps. In another example, a very troublesome buggane was described as "whirling like a spinning wheel" on top of a mountain. He then came to meet an old woman who had expressed the opinion that he ought to be chastened for his many pranks "whirring like a spinning wheel."[62]

Washing

The distinctive smell of the fairies was examined in the first chapter. The need for the fairies to wash themselves and their clothes, just like humans, was accepted without question by earlier generations of islanders. The saying was that "If rain falls when it's sunny, the fairies are washing."

An interesting account comes from the early twentieth century. A man reported that his father, when he was a boy, had come across the fairies doing their washing in the river at Glen Rushen. They were beating the clothes on the rocks and then hanging them to dry on gorse bushes. The boy crept close and stole a little cap, which

---

61 S. Morrison, 'Manx Dialect Connected with Fairies,' *Proceedings of the Isle of Man Natural History & Archaeological Society,* vol.1 (New Series), 1906; Waldron, *Isle of Man,* 38; Gill, *Manx Scrapbook,* c.4, 'Rushen;' F. Angwin, *Manx Folk Tales,* 71.

62 Broome, *Fairy Tales,* c.2 – 'Old Nance and the Buggane'.

was too small even for a human child to wear. He took it home to show his mother, but she told him to go straight back and replace it – which he did.[63]

The fairy women seem to prefer to do their laundry in groups; on the Rhenab River there was a large flat stone which was known as a spot where clothes were washed at night and early in the mornings. Other locations identified are Boayl ny Niee and, next to the Gretch River, a spot called the Fairy Ground where fairy mothers dressed in red used to be seen washing their babies. At Arbory, it used to be possible to hear the fairies beetling and bleaching their clothes by the stream and, in another location, children saw the fairies' newly washed garments spread out to dry on rocks in a deep glen one evening.[64]

Elder Trees

On the Isle of Man, the faeries' particular home is in elder trees (*tramman*). This shrub has the power to repel witches, as a result of which, according to Agnes Herbert's guide to the island written in 1909, there was hardly an old well (*tholtan* in Manx) to be found, near which there didn't grow an elder tree. If you carried elder leaves with you, the islanders believed, you would be protected against witchcraft. Puzzlingly, though, it is simultaneously believed that elder can also repel the fairies, as in the curious Manx custom of burying people, especially children, with a few leaves from the tree.[65]

These are but the first indications of the depth of the supernatural associations of the *tramman* tree on the island. When the branches

---

63 *Yn Lioar Manninagh*, vol.4, 161.
64 Gill, *Third Manx Scrapbook*, Part 2, c.3; *Yn Lioar Manninagh*, vol.2, 194–7; *Chambers Journal*, vol.3, 1855, 96.
65 Herbert, *The Isle of Man*, 1909, 194; A. W. Moore, *Folklore of the Isle of Man*, 1891, c.7; Gill, *Manx Scrapbook*, c.4 'Ballaugh'.

of the trees are seen to bend in the wind at night, this is a sign that the fairies riding upon them. Fairies' ears, or 'lugs,' (*cleeashyn hramman* – a type of fungus) are seen growing on elders; it is thought that to touch them is harmful.[66]

Given their status as fairy residences, interference with the trees can be extremely dangerous. Evans Wentz heard the story of a woman from Arbory parish on the island who, out walking one dark night, accidentally collided with a *tramman*. She was instantly struck by a terrible swelling, which all her neighbours agreed was the consequence of offending the fays by her clumsiness. In 1932 Manx folklorist Walter Gill recorded another local account that told of a man who cut down an elder – and was driven to suicide by the aggrieved fairies. When the elders at Ballaboy were felled, the fairies came at night to lament their loss. A large crowd assembled and fighting broke out amongst them. Severed fairy thumbs were found in the road the next morning as testimony to the violence. Similarly, if the trees become decayed and the best branches for swinging on fall off, the fairies will abandon a location.[67]

In general, in fact, the Manx fairies seem to spend a lot of their time up in trees. One summer evening a mother and daughter went down to a place on the Ballachrink river, called Lhingowl, to fetch their cows home. It was nearly sunset and they heard a lot of folk talking in the trees. They could distinguish between young and old, as well as the voices of children, and they seemed to be enjoying some joking, but (as mentioned in the last chapter) the pair couldn't understand a single word that was being said. The mother and daughter went closer to try to see who was up in the branches, but

---

66 Roeder, *Manx Folktales*, 1913, 3; *Mannin*, no.3, 1913; S. Morrison, 'Manx Dialect Connected with Fairies,' *Proceedings of the Isle of Man Natural History & Archaeological Society*, vol.1 (New Series), 1906.
67 Evans Wentz, *Fairy Faith*, 126; Walter Gill, *Second Manx Scrapbook*, 1932, c.5; *Proceedings of the Isle of Man Natural History & Archaeological Society*, vol.1, Jan.1889; *Manx Notes & Queries*, 1904, 125.

when they got near, they would hear the fairies in another place, and they went to five or six different places, but never got a glimpse of them. As a result, the mother said to her daughter that they had better drive the cows home, and get away as soon as possible, for it had to be the fairies. The girl said she had never liked to go down near Lhingowl again after that.[68]

Faery Hunts

On the Isle of Man faery hunts are a familiar part of the folklore; they closely resemble human foxhunts, with riders following packs of hounds across the countryside, although the Manx faery hunts are, predictably, almost always to be encountered at night. Repeated sightings at Port Erin and Port St Mary, but especially at Cronk Mooar, confirm that hunting was one of the particular pleasures of the *ferrishyn*. The faeries will be seen dressed up in red or green coats with flat red caps, accompanied by much cracking of whips, blowing of horns, the thunder of hooves and yelping of dogs. Witnesses have reacted differently to what they encountered: one man hid in a doorway and turned away his face so he could not see the pack passing; another, meanwhile, was so delighted by the sight of such "gallantly mounted" riders that he would happily have followed the hunt, had he been able to keep pace with them.[69]

Often humans' horses are taken from stables for this sport and are ridden without mercy through the night. They are found the next morning, sweating and foaming, back in their stalls. Waldron met one man from Ballafletcher would had lost four of his steeds through overexertion by the fairy hunt. Despite the harsh treatment

---

68 *Manx Notes & Queries,* 1904, 118.
69 Roeder, *Manx Folk Tales,* 5, 7 & 8; *Manx Notes & Queries,* 1904, 120; Moore, *Folklore,* c.3; Waldron, 30–39.

of many horses, there are apparently some that enjoy the thrill of racing with the fairy hunt. If they are left to graze loose in a field overnight, and the hunt passes nearby, the horse will escape to gallop with the hounds. If a person is unlucky enough to be riding such a steed at night, they may find themselves carried along in the wake of the hunt before finally being thrown.[70]

Once, the vicar of Bradda was seriously troubled by having his horse taken out of its field during the night, the animal being so misused that by the morning it would sweating all over and exhausted as if it had been furiously ridden for many miles. In spite of numerous enquiries in the neighbourhood, he could never learn who was doing this. However, early one morning he happened to be returning home from the bedside of a sick parishioner. Just as he was passing the horse's field, the reverend gentleman saw a little man in a green jacket, carrying a riding whip in his hand, who was in the act of turning the vicar's horse loose into the field. When the little man turned round and saw the human standing by the gate, he immediately vanished, and the saddle, which he had placed at the side of the fence, was turned into a stone in exactly the same shape. It has remained there ever since. It is almost needless to state that the vicar's horse was never molested again.[71]

Fairy Fleets

The Manx faeries have been said to have "unlimited influence over fishing" and to excel at the many crafts associated with the industry. Mostly, it is their sea fishing exploits that are recorded, but they also fish in the rivers of the island's glens.[72]

---

70   Waldron, *Description of the Isle of Man*, 33; Douglas, *Forgotten Dances*, 19.
71   Moore, *Folklore*, c.3.
72   D. Robertson, *A Tour Through the Isle of Man*, 1794, 75; *Manx Notes & Queries*, 1904, 116.

The fairies have been seen boat building at Perwick. One commentator dismissed these labours as mere imitation of humans, saying that they carry on the work at night, after the men have finished and gone home, as a sort of game – but without any noticeable result next morning. Nevertheless, given that faery fishing craft have been seen in use, this seems unfounded. In addition, the faeries have been spotted engaged in other preparations, such as mending nets and making barrels to store the catch of herring in. At Cronk-ny-Irree-Laa near Patrick there's a cave called Ooig-ny-Sieyr (the Cooper's Cave) in which the fairy barrel makers have been regularly heard at work. It's believed that to hear them (especially in May) promises good herring fishing for the faery fleets. However, good catches for the fairies can mean poor fishing for humans, and vice versa. Also, it's believed that to see their boats, or rather the innumerable twinkling lights of them, out at sea is either a sign that a good catch may be found there – or a warning to put in, because it presages a storm. Clearly the faeries' knowledge of the sea, fisheries and weather are greatly to be trusted.[73]

The fairies' boats have been seen on beaches after they have returned from a fishing trip and also being hauled to safety before a storm; they will frequently vanish very quickly once they know they've been seen. Their fleets are sometimes sighted out at sea in Peel Bay, illuminated by lanterns and with their nets and floats paid out, although hearing the sound of rowing and the splash of their oars is more common, because they will tend to extinguish their lights if they realise human boats are near. Another Manx witness described how he once saw fairies playing on beached fishing

---

[73] Gill, *Second Manx Scrapbook*, c.3 & *Third Manx Scrapbook*, c.3; *Yn Lioar Manninagh* vol.4, 161; Morrison, *Manx Fairy Tales*, 93, 'Little footprints;' *Manx Notes & Queries*, no.205; Gill, *Third Manx Scrapbook*, c.3; S. Morrison, 'Manx Dialect Connected with Fairies,' *Proceedings of the Isle of Man Natural History and Archaeological Society*, New Series vol.1, 1906.

boats, clambering about in the rigging with great laughter.[74]

Some of the doubt about the extent of the fairies' fishing enterprises must doubtless derive from their natural secrecy, meaning that they will tend to be active under cover of darkness, or otherwise concealed. For instance, a ship sailing to Whitehaven to fetch coals one night saw the sea full of lights as far as he could see. He concluded it was the fairies, out in their pleasure craft. In addition, it seems that the fairies will sometimes conceal the activities of their fishing fleets under dense mist. In the early 1900s one witness described how he had been sea-fishing from rocks when a fog approached over the sea. Then he heard what sounded like children's voices and found himself surrounded by fairy boats with lights on their prows and the men calling to each other in Manx.[75]

Lastly, the fairies of Glen Rushen used to keep their vessels in caves on the shore at the mouth of Glen Maye. A story is told of a battle that took place there between Manx and Irish fairies, the former being violently protective of their fishing grounds. This evidence of faery aggression leads us to our next subject.[76]

Fairy Fighting

Today, we tend to imagine fairies as being peaceable and contented beings, forever happy and engaged in pleasure. Previous generations, who had more contact with them, knew differently. I have just mentioned the fact that Manx fairies fought Irish incomers over access to fishing grounds, and there are a number of other examples that indicate their martial nature.

---

[74] *Yn Lioar Manninagh* vol.III, 482 & IV, 154–161; *Manx Notes and Queries*, 1904, 131; Morrison, *Manx Fairy Tales*, 1911, 'Little footprints'; *Manx Notes & Queries*, no.205; Roeder, *Manx Folk Tales*, 'Fairies of Sea & Shore;' *Manx Notes & Queries*, 1904, 158.
[75] *Yn Lioar Manninagh*, III, 182; Wentz 117-118.
[76] Gill, *Third Manx Scrapbook*, Part 2, c.3.

There is quite a bit of indirect evidence of the fairies' military preparedness. One witness, who became a member of the Manx Parliament, the House of Keys, was out walking one October night in 1830 when he and a friend saw a "great crowd of little beings smaller than Tom Thumb" who were dressed in red and organised in two and threes. They "moved back and forth… as they formed into order like troops drilling." In another case a man saw what he described as an 'army' dressed in red; in a third, two men met a fairy army on the road at Mull. They were all dressed in red caps and coats, some mounted, some on foot, and they so filled the highway that the men had to climb over the hedge and wait for quite some time for the host to pass. A fairy army is also mentioned in the story of 'Tom Beg and the Fairies.' Tom assists the fairy king by receiving the password from each of the six regiments that parade past him.[77]

Besides the account of the fairies fighting over their fishing grounds, there are other accounts of violence. Later I will describe an incident in which fairies fought amongst themselves over whether or not they should abduct a little girl. She was assaulted in the course of this and, when her relatives later went to the spot where she said events took place, they found blood spattered on the stones there.[78]

A final example demonstrates the fairies' bellicose nature even more clearly:

> "A woman walking over Barrule met two fairy armies going to battle, which was to begin on the ringing of a bell; she pulled the bell, and in consequence both armies attacked her, and kept her prisoner for three years, when she escaped."[79]

---

77 Wentz, 133; Bord, *Fairies*, 41 – 42; *Yn Lioar Manninagh* III; Roeder, *Manx Folktales*, 7; Morrison, *Manx Fairy Tales*, 56; 'One of Themselves for the Night' in F. Angwin, *Manx Folk Tales*, 2015, and see Broome, *More Fairy Tales*, 38.
78 Waldron, *Isle of Man*, 39.
79 *Choice Notes & Queries – Folklore*, 1859, 26.

Water Spirits

The coastal and inland waters of Man are inhabited by a surprising variety of supernatural beings, all of which are fascinating, but potentially deadly.

Mermaids

Given its long coastline, the inhabitants of the island, especially those who are involved in fishing, have had regular contact with the merfolk over the centuries and numerous stories are recorded. These are the well-known mermaids and mermen who are part human, part fish and are called *ben-varrey*. The females are said to be more numerous than the males; a few merchildren have even been seen. Two were found on rocks at the Calf of Man in 1810. One had already died; the other was saved and taken into Douglas town, where it was said to be about sixty centimetres in length, brown in colour except for violet scales on its tail and green coloured hair.[80]

On the shore under the Chasms near Cregneash, there is a pool which is filled with sea water at high tide, and fresh water on the ebb. The place is called Joan Mere's House and merfolk regularly used to be sighted there. One man reported seeing a male, who had a beard like a male human, along with female who had very long hair, white skin and very large breasts. When she saw the man spying, she slid down into the water, dragging herself along with her hands until she

---

80 *Manx Notebook,* vol.1, 1885, 'Some Ancient Manx Superstitions.'

could dive. Between Bow Veg and Glen Wither, on the coast north the Sound, there's a place called *Lhiondaig Pohllinag*, the Mermaid's Green or Garden, which was once frequented by mermaids who played and basked there.[81]

Whilst they may be seen sun bathing around the coast, the merfolk are reputed to have undersea homes where they breathe air like land dwellers. According to one account, an explorer in a diving bell who descended to a great depth found a grand city of houses and pyramids made of pearl and coral arranged around streets and squares.[82]

Most of our information about merfolk derives from their often-fraught interactions with humans, most of which are centred around sex and love. For example, at Niarbyl Bay a mermaid would regularly sing to the fishermen on the beach and eventually she won the heart of one and wed him. Mermaids are reputed to be very desirous of the love of humans and to actively pursue young men. Sometimes these relationships are relatively harmless: for example, one mermaid at Gob ny Ooyl seemingly fell for a man who curried favour with her by giving her apples, which she called the 'sweet land eggs;' his kindness brought him a wish of luck from the maid. At Casstruan the mermaids were said to have been very plentiful offshore and the local fishermen would befriend them by throwing them bread, butter and oatcakes.[83]

However, mermaids are always quite prepared to snatch away handsome fishermen. At Ballafletcher a mermaid fell in love with a shepherd and used to bring him bits of coral and pearls as a token of her affection. One day, as might have been predicted, she tried

---

81 *Manx Notes & Queries*, 197-9.
82 Moore, *Folklore*, c.4.
83 Roeder, *Manx Folktales*, Part One, 31; Gill, *Second Manx Scrapbook*, c.6; A. Herbert, *Isle of Man*, 183; *Manx Notebook*, vol.1, 1885, 'Some Ancient Manx Superstitions;' S. Morrison, *Manx Faery Tales*, 71 *Yn Lioar Manninagh*, vol.3 and vol1. Part 1, 290.

to drag him into the water but he resisted strongly and managed to escape her clutches. Angrily, she threw a stone after him and then disappeared. The blow he received was light, but he developed a severe pain in his bowels which killed him within a week. In another case, when the man rejected a mermaid's advances, the whole island suffered. She made a fog come down which either prevented ships leaving harbour or, if they dared to, led to them being wrecked on rocks and cliffs.[84]

The particular problem with mermaids is their notorious beauty. They are noted for their golden hair, their blue eyes and their sweet singing voices, which can reduce men to a sort of lovestruck daydreaming and which makes them neglect their family and their work. Men can become disastrously obsessed by mermaids, to the extent that they'll follow them into the sea, even though this will inevitably result in their deaths.[85]

Luckily, there seems to be a settled procedure for freeing a hapless fisherman from a mermaid's attentions. To do this he needs help from friends or family – and the right preparations. Herring roe has to be boiled for three days and then dried and ground into a powder. The human victim should consume this in a drink and then set to sea, protected by sprigs of vervain and a cross made of rowan wood. As soon as the mermaid appears and begins to follow her lover in the boat, a charm has to be repeated:

> "Ben-varrey, ben-varrey – go back to thy home,
> Til the sea from this island of Mannin doth roam,
> Find a mate with a tail, for if thou X should wed,
> In the deeps of the sea, he'll be drownded and dead."

---

[84] Waldron, *Isle of Man*, 65; Herbert, *Isle of Man*, 183; Moore, *Folklore*, c.4.
[85] Broome, *Fairy Tales*, 24–25 & 115–117.

As soon as this verse has been completed, the vervain should be dropped in the waves and an iron knife should be stuck in the mast, which will summon up a storm, driving the mermaid beneath the surface and the ship back to land.[86]

These perils notwithstanding, there can be friendly and helpful relationships between humans and merfolk. A stranded mermaid rescued from the beach and returned to the waves at Port Erin blessed her saviour's family and promised that every woman would have easy childbirths thenceforth. An identical tale is told of a mermaid found at Fleshwick in Rushen parish, except here the guarantee of safe deliveries was exacted by the human as the price of letting the captured mermaid go free.[87]

A merman who had been rescued from the shore used to express his gratitude by warning fishing boats of approaching storms. More generally, it's said that if a merman whistles, a storm is brewing and it is time to make for shore. If fishing boats crews were preparing herring on board ship, they always threw a share to the mermen in recognition of the help they gave and to keep on the right side of them.[88]

As this last example shows, help may be given purely voluntarily to humans. Some fishermen were once in their boats off Spanish Head when the sky started to darken. A mermaid rose above the waves and called out to them *"shiaull er thalloo"* ('sail to land'). Those who did were saved; those who didn't take her advice lost their tackle or, even, their lives.[89]

Mermaids can be a source of riches for humans, but this wealth is not always a blessing. One *ben-varrey* demonstrated her affection

---

86 Broome, *Fairy Tales,* 21–29.
87 *Yn Lioar Manninagh,* vol.III; W. Gill, *A Manx Scrapbook,*1929, c.4.
88 *Manx Notes & Queries,* 27 & 205; *Yn Lioar Manninagh,* vol.III
89 Davies, *Folklore of West Wales,* 144–5; Rhys, *Celtic Folklore,* vol.1, 163; Roeder, *Manx Folktales;* Gill, *Manx Scrapbook,* c.4, 'German.'

for the fisherman she fancied by leaving him shells and seaweed, but others can offer gifts a lot valuable more than this. In the story of the *Fisherman and the Ben-Varrey*, a poor fisherman sees a mermaid in a dream, who she advises him to dig near his house. He does so and finds a buried chest, "full of gold pieces of money, queer old coins with strange markings." He stops working, thinking he has become wealthy for the rest of his life, but the money turns out to be worthless to him, as everyone in the local town is suspicious and refuses to take the Spanish gold, so the man and his wife have precious metals – but no income to buy food. As is often the case, faery money can be a curse as well as a favour.[90]

A further problem with any relationship with a mermaid is the fact that, ultimately, she is quite alien to the human. It's not just the physical differences – the tail and the fact that the mermaids of the Isle of Man have web between their fingers; there is simply too much of a gulf between us in our ways of thinking about the world. For example, a mermaid caught in a fishing net was held captive for three weeks by the boat's crew. She refused to speak, eat or drink so that they finally relented and took her down to the beach to set her free. Other merfolk came to meet her at the sea's edge and when she was asked what men were like, she was overheard to say:

> "Very ignorant – they throw away the water eggs are boiled in."[91]

Another, who had become stranded on the beach as the tide went out at Balladoole near Castle Town called out to her rescuers, who had carried her back to the sea:

---

[90] Dora Broome, *Fairy Tales from the Isle of Man*, 1968, 115; contrast to this her story of 'The Merman's Coat' in *More Fairy Tales from the Isle of Man*, 1970, 1, in which the gold paid by the merman for his coat enriches a whole village.
[91] Roeder, *Manx Folktales*, Part One, *Yn Lioar Manninagh*, III; Train, *A Historical and Statistical Account of the Isle of Man*, (Douglas: M. Quiggin, 1845), c.XVIII.

"One butt in Ballacreggan is worth all of Balladoole."

It may be possible to extract some sense from this, if the 'butt' refers to a barrel of fish. If this is right, she may have been saying that the herring catch at the first location would always be better than that off the beach where she was found – a helpful hint for the men who saved her. It's also quite possible that she made reference to smuggling – possibly suggesting that a barrel of brandy landed at Ballacregan was worth the entire fishing village.[92]

It's plain that merfolk need to be treated with cautious respect. Wise sailors know that, when they're out at sea, they should never refer to them by the names used on land, so that the mermaid, the *ben-varrey* or *pohllinagh*, is called instead *Joaney Gorm* ('Blue Joan'), a habit which must be linked to the name taboo so often found in folklore accounts. In just the same way, when at sea, sailors referred to the merman as the 'little boy,' *yn guilley beg*, and made offerings of oatbread and butter to him. It's very evidently inadvisable to annoy or hurt a mermaid – indeed, it's said that if you vex a *ben varrey*, you will never again have any luck when you're out fishing.[93]

Other Marine Spirits

One Manx story involves a man deliberately seeking out a mermaid bride for himself, though the spouse he ends up with seems to be much more like the seal-like being called a 'selkie' in the Scottish Highlands. A farmer had heard great praise for the beauty and charm of the merwomen and had resolved that he would only marry a mermaid. He sent one of his farm servants to the beach

---

92 Rhys, *Celtic Folklore*, vol.1, 166; *Yn Lioar Manninagh*, vol.III; Roeder, *Manx Folktales*, Part One.
93 S. Morrison, 'Manx Dialect Connected with Fairies,' *Proceedings of the Isle of Man Natural History & Archaeological Society*, vol.1 (New Series), 1906; *Manx Notes & Queries*, 1904, no.27.

to catch one and bring her home. The servant went and watched them nine times before he was able to ambush one when she was too far away from the magical sealskin she had taken off to be able to escape back into the sea. People warned the farmer to ensure she could never get her skin back again, or he would lose her for ever. He hid it away in an unused room in his house that was always kept locked. Years afterwards, when they were spring-cleaning, the seal skin got turned out, and the wife found it, put it on, and instantly vanished into the sea.[94]

The Manx people used to sacrifice rum to the *buggane* of Kione Dhoo headland, which looked something like a horse. A noggin of the spirit would be poured into the sea by fishing boats from Port St Mary as they passed the promontory on their way to the Kinsale and Lerwick fishing grounds. The object of their sacrifice was a cave called *Ghaw-Kione-dhoo* (Black Head Inlet). Rum was occasionally thrown from the top of the cliff as well, with the words '*Gow shen y veisht*' "Take that, evil spirit (or monster)!". This dedication resembles that which accompanied the fish thrown to the merfolk at sea "*Gow shen, dooinney varrey!*" ('Take that, sea people.')[95]

Manx people also believe in a more general sea spirit called the *cughtagh* who may be heard singing to himself in caves. This being has a voice that sounds like waves and seems to be related to the *bugganes* of the island as well as to the Scottish Gaelic *ciudach*, a cave dwelling giant or monster.[96]

---

[94] Gill, *Manx Scrapbook,* c.4, 'Patrick.'
[95] Gill, *Third Manx Scrapbook,* c.2, s.6.
[96] C. Roeder, *Manx Folktales,* 31; Gill, *Second Manx Scrapbook,* c.6; A. Herbert, *Isle of Man,*1909, 183; *Manx Notebook,* vol.1, 1885, 'Some Ancient Manx Superstitions.'

Fresh Water Spirits

There are reports of 'white ladies' who emerge from the sea at Germans and Michael and have married local men. These seem to be some sort of mermaid or selkie, rather than a sprite coming out of a body of water onto the land. To add to the confusion, there are several Manx spectres in pale silk robes seen flitting around wells who also bear this label. One in white silk is often encountered near Lewaigue Bridge and may waylay passers-by or enter people's homes. In a very similar incident, a man travelling from Ramsey to Laxey once met with a greyish woman accompanied by a low shaggy dog. At first, they approached each other along the road in the normal manner but, before they met and passed each other, the woman and dog suddenly vanished, leaving the man feeling weak and trembling. In another strange 'white lady' story, the ghostly female was seen nightly after dark near a farm. Then, one night, a servant looked out of the window at night and saw a doll hopping around the building before knocking three times on the door; she was so frightened that she couldn't pull herself back into the room without the help of other servants. The house was suddenly illuminated – and then plunged into darkness. These 'white ladies' have been seen at a variety places around the island and the understandable consensus is that it's best to avoid water courses and deep valleys at night because of them.[97]

The term 'white ladies' is also applied to the female fairy lovers, the *lhiannan shee* (see later), and to various other spectral or ghostly women who have been encountered across the island and who share some of the traits of the *lhiannan*. These are often silent, but will follow men wordlessly until they bless themselves or use a holy

---

[97] Gill, *Second Manx Scrapbook*, c.6, section 2; *Choice Notes & Queries – Folklore*, 1859, 26.

name. An illustration comes from Kay's Bridge in Patrick parish. It is, or was, haunted by a white fairy or ghost a little smaller than human size, who used to follow people silently along the road.[98]

At Kebeg, there is a pool along the Ballacoan stream which is inhabited by a *nyker,* a type of water faery. A beautiful cow girl was once abducted into river by this sprite. People heard her calling her cows near the pool, but then a mist descended, a voice was heard replying to her calls – and she was never seen again. Another *nyker*, in the form of a horse or pony, or sometimes a handsome young man, is known to haunt the pond called Nikkesen's Pool in Lonan Parish. In male form, this *nikkesen* sings a beautiful but mournful song in an unknown tongue, with which he tries to tempt girls into the water with him. If a young woman enters his pool, her body is never found again; instead, on moonlit nights, the *nikkesen* may be seen near the pool dancing in a circle with his victims. Dangerous as these spirits are, they luckily never seem to stray beyond the banks of their pools.[99]

Lastly, the spirit called Jenny the Whinney on the island is akin to Jenny Greenteeth on the mainland: she is a creature who haunts rivers and pools and tries to drag in people on the bank, most especially unwary children. There was also a creature called the crogan, a female water spirit, that haunted multiple spots around the island. She is largely forgotten now and her characteristics and habits seem to have been lost.[100]

---

98 *Manx Notes & Queries,* 1904, 134–137, 142 & 180–181; Gill, *Manx Scrapbook,* c.4, 'Patrick.'
99 Morrison, *Manx Faery Tales,* 83; Gill, *Manx Scrapbook,* c.4; Douglas, 18.
100 Gill, *Manx Scrapbook,* c.4.

Water Bulls

The water bull may be best known in Scotland, but on the Isle of Man this supernatural animal is very widely found as well, being called the *tarroo ushtey*. It is the subject of considerable folklore and we know a great deal about the beast.

A *tarroo* was well known during the 1830s at Slieu Mayll, a fierce creature with fiery eyes. It moved about very slowly and with a strange whirring noise; one farmer broke his stick hitting it when he tried to drive it along. Another example was spotted slightly more recently in 1859, in the vicinity of Ballure Glen, and people travelled from all over the island to be able to see it. This *tarroo* was said to be small and dark but, overall, not very different in appearance from a normal bull. Some witnesses have compared the *tarroo* to a bear; others say that it whilst it is normally black, the bull can change its colour to blend in with a herd in a field. Water bulls are chiefly recognised by their shining coats and sharp ears.[101]

As a species, the *tarroo* can live in both salt and fresh water. It prefers river pools and bogs, although one was seen on a pebble bank on the beach at Port Cornaa. If a bull is sighted at all, it will be either early in the morning or towards evening and it will seldom be alone, but nearly always amongst a herd of cows. By way of illustration, at Booilley Grongan in Maughold, a boy saw a calf in the fields running after the cows. He told his father, the farmer, because there had been no calf expected in the herd. They realised it was likely to have been a *tarroo* playing amongst the heifers. The persistent presence of a *tarroo* in the area was indicated by the fact that a local pond was called *Dem ny tarroo ushtey*.[102]

---

[101] *Isle of Man Times*, Nov.28th 1888, 4, 'Antique Mona;' Herbert, *Isle of Man*, 187; M. Douglas, *Forgotten Dances*, 19; Gill, *Third Manx Scrapbook*, Part 2, c.3.
[102] *Manx Notebook*, vol.1, 1885, 'Some Ancient Manx Superstitions;' M. Douglas, *Forgotten Dances*, 19; Gill, *Third Manx Scrapbook*, Part 2, c.3.

It's believed that the water bulls were dangerous to other cattle – not deliberately by devouring them but because of their interest in the cows, with which they always seek to mate. They may also try to lure cows away into the nearest river or lake. For example, in June 1888, a *tarroo* was seen at dawn in the fields around Lhanjaghan. The bull in a farmer's herd reacted to its appearance violently, charging the intruder, bellowing and demolishing a fence in its rage. The *tarroo* was indifferent, though, and simply cantered calmly away and plunged off a cliff into the river, where it floated around placidly for a while before roaring and then diving. Admittedly, the *tarroo* will sometimes mutilate or kill bullocks in herds when competing over mates, but they are too quick and nimble for farmers ever to catch them and prevent the depredations. It's reported that at Granane in Lonan parish a very large and ferocious *tarroo* used to mutilate the farm's bullocks, so an adult Spanish bull was brought in to try to defend the livestock. However, when the two fought, the *tarroo* quickly vanquished its competitor and gored the new bull to death.[103]

Especially around May Day, the water bulls are prone to get in amongst the farmers' herds to try to mate with the cows, but the results of the *tarroo* interbreeding with regular cattle are highly undesirable, as the cows will either abort or will give birth to calves that are misshapen monsters, comprising skin and flesh without bones.[104]

Generally, the bulls are good natured, often being seen playing in meadows, and they are mostly harmless to humans, being shy of them and tending to avoid their proximity as much as possible. Nonetheless, there was apparently one farmhouse at Granane near

---

[103] *Isle of Man Times,* Nov.28th 1888, 4, 'Antique Mona;' M. Douglas, *Forgotten Dances,* 19; Train, *Isle of Man,* vol.2, c.XVIII; Gill, *Second Manx Scrapbook,* c.6(4).

[104] Waldron, *Isle of Man,* 43; Train, *Isle of Man,* vol.2, c.XVIII; Leney, *Shadowland in Ellan Vannin,* 143; Rhys, *Manx Folklore,* Part One.

the Laxey River in Lonan that was abandoned because of the presence of the local *tarroo*. The beast used to come up from the river bed to roar around the house, apparently trying to get in by battering at the entrances with its horns. The inhabitants had to barricade the shutters and doors with their heaviest furniture and were awoken every night by the noise and by their own fear. They eventually were driven away from the place. The best protection for herds from the attentions of the *tarroo* is to make crosses of rowan and to tie them to the cattle's tails or attach them to the lintels of stables and cattle sheds. Alternatively sprays of rowan might be scattered around.[105]

The water bulls may not threaten people directly, but they can be deeply alarming because of their bellowing and because of their ability to change their size. For example, Chibbert y Vull, a roadside well at Ballakillowey, Rushen, is haunted by a *tarroo*. It was seen by one witness who described how [with] "every jump it made it would be growing, when it was coming out of the well; it would grow large and go after the cows. One of these bulls came into the Ballacurrey fields, and began to go after the cattle . . . "[106]

The Manx bulls are loud and large and certain locations are avoided during the hours of darkness in consequence. As an example of the fear the *tarroo* can instil, two boys who'd been out stealing apples at Cronk Leannag were on their way home when they came face to face with a huge bull with blazing eyes the size of cups. It charged them and they fled, after which it plunged into a swamp and was gone.[107]

The Manx water bull seems strong and insuperable but, as we have seen, herbal charms can quite easily overcome it. A further

---

105 *Manx Notes & Queries,* 1904, no.96; Gill, *Manx Scrapbook.* c.4 – Lezayre; Douglas, *Forgotten Dances,* 20; Leney, *Shadowland in Ellan Vannin,* 143; Moore, *Folklore,* c.7.
106 Gill, *Manx Scrapbook,* c.1; *Yn Lioar Manninagh,* 1897, 166.
107 Moore, *Folklore,* c.4; *Yn Lioar Manninagh,* vol.4; I. Leney, *Shadowland in Ellan Vannin,* 144; J. Rhys, *Manx Folklore and Superstition,* Part One; Train, *Isle of Man,* vol.2, c.18; Gill, *Second Manx Scrapbook,* c.6.

report has suggested that, whilst sticks and pitchforks were no match for it, a shotgun or rifle would be effective. Such extreme force didn't always seem to be needed, though. There was once a *tarroo ushtey* that lived in a pool where the promenade at Ramsey now runs; it used to roar and splash in the water and disturb people living nearby. It threatened a local man one time and he raised his stick as if to strike it, but then thought better of striking it and pulled his blow. All the same, this was found to have been enough to have rendered the beast powerless.[108]

At Chibber Pooyl Sallagh, on the north-east slopes of Cronk ny Irree Lhaa in Patrick parish, a man called Pharick y Kellya was cutting turf one summer evening in the 1820s when he saw a little *tarroo* rising out of the well. As he watched, it grew bigger and bigger and then began to advance towards him. In his alarm, Pharick set about the beast with his *faayl* (turf-spade), until there was nothing left at all but a soft jelly, like frog-spawn.[109]

These two subjugations of a bull by blows contrast strongly with our final story. A farmer found a *tarroo* amongst his herd and unwisely struck it with his stick, causing the bull to bolt and plunge wildly into the sea. This quickly brought a blight on the man's grain crops, but he did not learn his lesson. When he found the bull grazing with his herd a second time, he tried to catch it, but the *tarroo* escaped. A further blight fell, this time on his potato crop. Although the farmer was advised to show greater respect for supernatural livestock, he was not to be lectured and the next time the bull appeared, he was ready: using a rowan stick he drove the *tarroo* into a shed and penned it there. On the next market day, the bull was driven into town with the rowan stick, but most people realised what it was and made no offers of purchase. Late in the day

---

108 Gill, *Second Manx Scrapbook*, c.6 & *Third Manx Scrapbook*; Waldron, *Isle of Man*, 43; Roeder, *Manx Folktales,* Part One.
109 Gill, *Manx Scrapbook*, c.1.

a man expressed interest, but only if the farmer rode the beast, as he boasted he easily could – because it was so docile and obedient. The foolhardy farmer climbed onto the *tarroo's* back and, at first, all went well – until the rowan wand fell from his grasp – at which point the beast galloped off into the sea with the farmer clinging on desperately. He survived this ordeal – but was very much chastened.[110]

The *tarroo ushtey* was once a highly disturbing presence all over the Isle of Man but, fortunately perhaps, drainage on the island has much diminished the number of water bulls that are sighted today, as many of the marshes they once infested have disappeared.[111]

Water Horses

On the Isle of Man, there are two horse-like faery beasts, the *cabbyl ushtey* (water horse) and the *glashan*. The water horse lives both in rivers and in the sea. It has been called a 'furious beast' because it poses a constant threat to the islanders' livestock, as it will emerge from watercourses and rip cattle to pieces or it will chase ponies across the mountains; sometimes it even carries off children. For example, on the Awn Dhoo near Greeba Mill in German, a farmer's wife once was out grazing her cows by the river. One went missing and the only trace found of it was some tufts of hair on the river bank. The next day, her husband took the cattle out. He heard a splashing and trampling and a monstrous creature arose from the river, seized a calf, and tore it to pieces. A little while later, the couple's daughter also disappeared – after which the herd was troubled no longer by the beast.[112]

---

110 Broome, *Fairy Tales*, c.16.
111 J. Rhys, *Manx Folklore and Superstition*, Part One.
112 Gill, *Manx Scrapbook*, 226; *Aberdeen Journal*, Sept.11th 1886, 8 'Manx Bogies.'

In the parish of Lonan, a *cabbyl ushtey* or *cabbyl vooar* (big horse) has frequently been seen at twilight on the sea-shore or on the tracks leading up the cliffs from the beach. It is said to be white or dun coloured (never grey like the *glashtyn*) and it can travel as easily on (or under) the sea as upon the land. It may carry off unwary riders who mount it, but these victims do not drown when they are plunged into the waves, but find that they can breathe underwater. The *cabbyl* might, very occasionally, consent to being haltered and used by farmers; when it dies so, it's found to be it's very strong and useful, easily hauling up loads of seaweed from the beaches to fertilise the fields.[113]

The *cabbyl* is a white or brown in colour and there are said to be several living in bodies of fresh water across the island, in marshy places, deep pools, basins in river beds, behind waterfalls and in lakes. The *cabbyl* has been accused of being a 'foul thief' because, if it meets lone travellers at night, it will try to lure them into its pool. However, the beast can be tamed with a special bridle which has been decorated with yarrow, woodbine, rowan, fern and rosemary; then a circle is drawn around the horse and charms recited.[114]

The second type of 'water horse' found on Man is the *glashan*, which derives its name from the Manx *glas*, denoting its grey colouring. There is considerable confusion between the *glashan* and the bogie or hob-like *glashtyn*, who undertakes heavy labour on farms, but is also, curiously, known to appear in the guise of a water horse that lurks in pools and rivers. One local called it a water goblin – half cow and half horse. The fact that there are two beasts with very similar names living in identical habitats makes it is very difficult to distinguish the two, although some writers have attempted to do so. Because separating the creatures is so difficult,

---

113 Gill, *Manx Scrapbook,* 226; Douglas, *Forgotten Dances*, 19.
114 *Manx Notes & Queries,* 1904, no.93; Rhys, *Manx Folklore,* Part One.

I will treat the *glashan* and the horse-form of the *glashtyn* are being the same thing. In the form of a dark grey colt, the *glashan/glashtyn* is found in several locations across the island, haunting boggy fields and pools and emerging at night onto meadows and lake banks. Despite his very poor reputation, the beast luckily never strays too far from the immediate vicinity of his stream or pool. Still, the *glashtyn* that used to live in a marshy area near Ballagorry Chapel could be heard at night tearing up and down the field where it lived, keeping people nearby awake.[115]

The *glashan*, and the *glashtyn* in horse form, both seem to be quite small, and there are no reports of it posing a serious threat to either livestock or humans; instead, in the shape of a one-year-old lamb it would get amongst the flocks in the fold and cause mischief, but no harm. The water horse has definitely been known to give people a fright by galloping off with them on its back if they are foolhardy enough to mount it. Luckily, unlike the Scottish equivalents, to which people find themselves stuck, it's possible to jump clear of these Manx beasts. Nonetheless, it's plainly best to avoid a severe shock, so the advice is as follows. If you ever come across a solitary horse on the island, examine it carefully before getting too close. If it has human ears, you're dealing with a water horse. That said, one example of the breed at Glen Maye is believed to have a human body but a horse's ears and hooves. A minister who mounted such a steed was able to escape by crying out 'Lord help me!' He was then thrown off onto the grassy verge. The *glashtyn* can be nuisance too: for instance, two tried to steal pork from a butcher's cart once. The man driving the van had to hold them off with his whip all night, until at dawn they vanished.[116]

---

[115] Wentz, 131; *Manx Notebook*, vol.1, 1885, 'Some Ancient Manx Superstitions;' Gill, *Third Manx Scrapbook*, Part 2, c.3; *Manx Notes & Queries*, 1904, 93 & 98.

[116] Gill, *Manx Scrapbook*, c.4, 'Patrick; J. F. Campbell, *Popular Tales*, vol.1, xlvi; Douglas, *Forgotten Dances*, 18; *Yn Lioar Manninagh*, vol.3, 134.

Unlike the *tarroo ushtey*, the *glashan/ glashtyn* is said to mingle with the herds of mountain ponies or with the horses kept by Manx farmers without any disturbance or hostility between the animals. However, the water horses only liked to mate with pure Manx-bred ponies and, as the island's horses interbred more and more with outside breeds, their supernatural companions were seen less and less.[117]

We shall return to discuss the *glashtyn* in its human form at the end of the next chapter.

Other Water Sprites

As will already be clear, there is a strong association between Manx faeries and water sources. A number of wells have been visited by islanders for both the benefits they bestowed and the protection that they gave against fairies and witches. For example, those drinking the waters of the well at Croggan would leave pins, buttons or silver as payment to the fairies for their help and healing. At other springs, more elaborate rituals were involved, such as circling the well sunwise before drinking and making an offering, even if it was only a pebble.[118]

In point of fact, numerous 'fairy wells' are identified on the island, a couple of which are even named as such – '*chibber y ferrishyn*.' These are guarded by female spirits, such as the woman seen first in a brown shawl and then later in yellow shining silk who sang for hours at Thalloo Holt, Slieu Rea. The well at Chibber na Gabbyl was the site of a fairy fair; at Chibber Vreeshey fairy music could be heard, at Chibber Feeayr there was a Green Lady whilst Glen Cutchery well's water had magic properties that helped butter

---
117 *Isle of Man Times,* Nov.28th 1888, 4, 'Antique Mona.'
118 Jenkinson, *Practical Guide to the Isle of Man,* 75; Gill, *Manx Scrapbook,* c.1.

to churn (whilst the water from some other wells could actively impede the process). One Manx informant believed that the 'wine' drunk at fairy feasts was in fact water from one of these wells and that, if a human drank it, s/he would fall into the fairies' power for ever.[119]

The islanders identified their own faery washer women akin to the banshees and *bean nighe* of the Scottish Highlands. These beings were conceived as a kind of *lhiannan-shee* (a vampiric faery lover), being seen in the form of a small woman who would be found washing clothes in a stream, always dressed in red. She would beat the laundry with a *sladdan* (stick/ mallet) or on the river rocks, sometimes using one hand only whilst in the other she held a candle; on other occasions, the candle might be seen stuck into the earth of the river bank. The appearance of the little red washer woman was always a sign of bad weather approaching.[120]

A similar sprite called the *dooiney-oie* or 'night caller' performs the same function. He's sometimes seen as a man in long dark coat with shining buttons and a wide brimmed hat and he has been called a 'banshee,' because he sometimes seems attached to a single family, although he doesn't predict an imminent death as the Scottish being does. Rather, if the *dooiney-oie*'s dismal howls of 'Hoa! Hoa!' are heard during a winter's night on the coast, it's a sure sign that storms are approaching across the Irish Sea. Because of his warnings, the Manx people have regularly avoided considerable loss: fishermen have been able to get in their nets, lines and pots and farmers could shelter their flocks. The *dooiney-oie* has even been said to perform some farm work, but his main occupation is undoubtedly to keep a look out for bad weather and blowing his horn. Famously, a man who was disturbed by the *dooiney-oie* sounding his warnings hid

---

119 Gill, *Manx Scrapbook*, c.1; *Second Mona Miscellany* 194.
120 Gill, *Third Manx Scrapbook*, c.2.

the horn, leading to a serious quarrel between them and the night caller disappearing in a sulk for several years.[121]

The night-caller has been associated with a number of locations around the island, such as the glen at Ballaconnell in Malew parish and a cave on Cronk-y-Thonna. People tended to avoid him – and for good reason. As with all faery beings, it is wise not to affront him: some men who once insulted the *dooiney-oie* promptly found themselves pelted with stones from an invisible source and any group of boys who have tried to creep up to his cave to get a glimpse of him invariably end up with sprained wrists and ankles – after which, they tended to learn their lesson. The worst injury he can inflict, all the same, is the shock caused by his very loud shouting.[122]

---

121 Broome, *Fairy Tales*, c.10.
122 Train, *Isle of Man*, vol.2, c.18; Gill, *Manx Scrapbook*, c.4 – Malew; Moore, *Folklore*, c.3; Morrison, "Dooiney-oie," *Folklore* vol.23 (1912), 342; Jenkinson, *Practical Guide*, 40.

Manx Bogies and Goblins

On Man there are a several different bogies or goblins. Charles Roeder put them in a wider British context by comparing the *fynoderee* to hobs and brownies and the *bugganes* to pucks and *bwccas*. The difference between the Manx species can be a little hard to discern: even Manx folklore expert Walter Gill referred to the "confused tribes of *glashtyns, fenoderees* and *bugganes* of various descriptions."[123]

Bugganes

The Isle of Man equivalent to the bogie or boggart of the British mainland is the *buggane*. Like many of their species, they have been described as "polymorphous creatures." Walter Gill explains that "the name in fact covers almost all apparitions of the gloomier sort, black dogs in particular, and even ghosts when these are not recognisably human." They have a "native elasticity and adaptability." Bugganes are great shapeshifters and can be encountered in many widely varying forms: as a strong man with big eyes, as a black bear-like monster, as little stacks of hemp or corn or as sacks of chaff. One looks like a goat with a loud bleat, another like a little white pig that swells up to

---

[123] Gill, *Manx Scrapbook*, c.4, 'Marown.'

the size of a bull; one resembles a heifer without head or tail, another a whote collie dog wearing a white collar. There is a buggane that appears as a black monster the size of a haystack that fills the entire width of a road; a second is a hybrid being that's a man with a horse's head and glowing eyes. They may also appear as hares, calves, pigs or as black cats – albeit ones that might suddenly swell up to look as big as a horse or could shapeshift, for example from a pig to a heifer to a dog and then back again. The cry of the buggane has been described as "being something between the bellowing of a bull and a man being choked." Evidently, with such a range of appearances, it can prove difficult to determine exactly what sort of supernatural being you may be confronted by. The *bugganes*' main habit is to assault, threaten or follow travellers, or to block their passage along a road, although luckily a blessing or some other holy words, or speaking one true thing, will dispel them. One buggane, in the form of a large horse that seemed set to trample and devour a Methodist minister, vanished in a flash of fire when he knelt and began to pray.[124]

Bugganes are invariably mischievous, if not malicious. At the least, they can be eerie and unsettling beings. One was often seen between Ballagawne and Ballcurrie, sometimes looking like a pig, sometimes like a man in officer's clothes. He is said once to have followed a mother and son home and then stood looking in at the window when they were in bed. The woman found that, if she put the boy on the opposite side of the bed, the buggane vanished; if he lay by the wall, the being reappeared. In January 1872 it was speculated that workmen may have abandoned the site of road improvements at Ballanard Hill, Onchan, because a buggane had appeared to them and remonstrated against the disturbance they were causing.[125]

---

[124] Gill, *Manx Scrapbook*, c.2 & *Second Manx Scrapbook* c.6; Roeder, *Manx Folk Tales*, Part One; *Yn Lioar Manninagh*, vol.2, 197 & vol.3, 134; *Manx Notes & Queries*, 1904, 97, 169, 171–177 & 184.

[125] *Manx Notes & Queries*, 1904, no.13; *Isle of Man Times*, Jan.6th 1872, 3.

Even odder and more puzzling variants of the *buggane* are reported from around the island. One travels around in a form resembling a spinning wheel, laughing all the while at humans' misfortunes. Sometimes, *bugganes* can be entirely shapeless, just a black mist that engulfs and chokes a person. In Malew parish, the 'Big Buggane' was once seen looking like a large man shining all over, as if he was dressed in an oil skin coat. At Grenaby, the *buggane* called Jimmy Squarefoot has a pig's head and face with two large tusks and has been known to charge at passers-by on the highway and even to carry off people to a cave. Another 'pig *buggane*' menaces travellers on the highway at Lezayre. Some of the species live in sea caves: the one at Ghaw ny Spyrryd has three horns and a head as big as pot. The Kione Dhoo (black head) *buggane* takes the form of a horse with eyes like plates; it gallops about howling and rattling chains. Walter Gill prefers to describe this particular example as a "shore-haunting sea-demon who appears as a horse, or something partially resembling one" rather than as a *buggane*. Gob-ny-scuit gully in Maughold parish is haunted by a *buggane* that appears in several shapes: as a large man with a cat's head and fiery eyes, as a man with a horned head and bright eyes or as a giant male dripping with blood. He howls at night and his breath is a noisome vapour.[126]

The last example cited is renowned for being an especially mischievous creature, for it likes to vex the locals. It will tear the thatch off haystacks, blow smoke back down chimneys, deposit soot in the inhabitants' food, and push sheep over the edge of cliffs. Lastly, at Spooyt Moor in Patrick parish, there is a *buggane* that tends to be seen as a big black calf which will cross the road in front of travellers, alarming them with the sounds of chains being rattled, and then plunges into a pool. In his human form this *buggane* tried

---

126 Gill, *Manx Scrapbook*, c.2, 'Malew;' *Mannin*, no.5, 1914; Douglas, *Forgotten Dances*, 21; *Manx Notes & Queries*, 1904, no.97.

once to abduct a local girl; he threw her over his shoulder and carried her off towards his lair, which was the cave behind a nearby waterfall, but she was luckily able to cut the strings of her apron and escape his clutches.[127]

There is apparently quite a strong moralistic streak in at least some of these creatures. The *buggane* of Glen Maye tried to throw a lazy housewife into a waterfall because she had delayed her baking until after sunset. Had she not cut loose the strings of her apron to escape, she would at the very least have had an icy soaking. The *buggan ny Hushtey* lived in a large cave near the sea and likewise had no liking for idle people, it was said. Nonetheless, this work ethic was paired with a sense of pity for the less fortunate. When Poor Robin of nearby Chou Traa lost his faithful dog and a barrel full of buttermilk through a cruel prank, the *buggane* took care of him by bringing in the cows, lighting the fire and boiling the kettle, ready for when he came home. The loss of the company of his dog at the same time made Robin depressed, so that he slept poorly, got up late and fell behind with his farm tasks. Late one evening when he was still out in the field ploughing by the light of a lantern, the *buggane* made the plough horse bolt through a hedge. It was found dead the next day, near to the entrance to the *buggane*'s cave – and this provoked the villagers into blocking the hole and then placing a stone cross there to bar the *buggane*'s passage.[128]

For all this criticism, some manifestations of the *buggane* are helpful to humans; there is a very clear cross-over here with the *dooiney-oie* whom I mentioned in the last chapter. The being that lived in *Towl Buggane* (the Buggane's Hole) at Gob-ny-Scuit would shout a warning before stormy weather, enabling local farmers to get

---

127 Gill, *Manx Scrapbook,* c.4 & *Third Manx Scrapbook,* c.3; Douglas, *Forgotten Dances,* 21.
128 S. Morrison, *Manx Fairy Tales,* 10; Morrison, "The buggane ny hushtey – a Manx folktale," *Folklore,* vol.34, (1923), 349.

in their harvests in time. He was just as likely, though, to give these warnings when no storms were due, just to tease the locals. The Big Buggane or *Buggane Moar* was a frightening looking being, pitch black in colour, who lived in caves on South Barrule and Snaefell. However, he was generally seen at night when there was a storm approaching, acting as a warning to islanders. He would also help busy farmers thrash their corn but, once again, if he considered them to be lazy, he would do the work, take the grain and leave just the 'offal' or husks behind.[129]

The buggane seen at Ballakillingham was fairly representative of its kind in that it appeared as a large grey bulldog with an awful howl. It would lurk in the shadows, alarming travellers (much like the black dogs to be discussed later). However, this particular spirit had another quality. If your pig was sickly, collecting dust from where the *buggane* walked at night and rubbing it on the pig's back (along with saying the right charm) would heal the animal.[130]

However moralistic *bugganes* may be on their own terms, they strongly dislike churches and chapels and will demolish them. The *buggane* at St Trinian objected to the building of the saint's church on the slopes of Greeba Mountain. Three times, it ripped the roof off the building, so that the church was never completed. This specimen is wrinkly black, as big as a house, and with green hair and blazing eyes, but he can also shape-shift, shrinking to the size of a beetle or a mouse, appearing like a large, dark calf or tearing off his head and throwing it at people like a blazing ball. The *buggane* at Keeil Pharick has been described literally as a demon, having a big head, long arms, sharp claws and cloven feet.[131]

---

129 Gill, *Third Manx Scrapbook*, Part 2, c.3; *Isle of Man Times*, January 21st 1889, 3 'Antique Mona;' Broome, *Fairy Tales*, 53–57.
130 *Mannin*, no.7, 1916.
131 Morrison, *Manx Folk Tales*, 153; *Manx Notes & Queries*, 1904, no.97; Broome, *Fairy Tales*, 101.

The suggestion of connections between *bugganes,* the devil and hell are reinforced in the case of the *buggane* of The Smelt, which is believed to be the ghost of a murdered man. He was often seen sitting on a stile; one old woman who wanted to get past recited the Lord's prayer, which made him vanish. Another time, a man was too terrified to pass but the *buggane* spoke to him reassuringly saying "if you don't molest me, I won't molest you."[132]

There is a strong belief that connects bugganes to those who have been murdered or who have died unfairly. They seem to be the ghosts of those who have died without receiving justice – including, in one case, a man from Slieauwhallin who was wrongfully executed for a murder he did not commit. Although they are generally said to inhabit caves, the *bugganes* that are some sort of ghost will tend to be found haunting the site of their death. Indeed, it's said that there are hardly any *bugganes* any longer because so few murders are committed anymore, so there aren't the unsettled ghosts wandering the earth seeking vengeance.[133]

Various brave but foolhardy Manx men have tried to fight *bugganes* – almost always without success. The beings' strength, and their ability to change size and shape, makes them nearly impossible to defeat. Luckily, they're not very bright and can fairly easily be outwitted and beaten. The best way of dealing with one is to speak the absolute truth to it – something it apparently respects.

Bugganes make it dangerous to be out at night and have caused great fear to the island population. In light of the idea that they may be demons, or spirits of the dead, it is understandable that a willow cross is considered to protect against them (and *fynoderees* too) although how much efficacy derives from the wood and how much from the religious significance of the shape, can't be determined

---

132 *Manx Notes & Queries,* 1904, no.10; Broome, *Fairy Tales,* 69–73.
133 *Mona Miscellany,* 2nd series, 21, 1873, 260; *Mannin,* no.5, 1914, 'Creignish Folklore Notes.'

conclusively.[134] As mentioned, other effective remedies are to pray or to simply cross a hedge to escape the creature, but the shock of meeting a *buggane* can prostrate a person for months, leave them mentally ill for life – or even kill them.[135]

Given that *bugganes* are "responsible for all manner of bad luck" and are a constant presence at various sites in the Manx landscape, it is understandable that communities may seek more permanent solutions to the threat they pose. Rather like ghosts, they can be 'laid' or exorcised. For example, a local newspaper reported in 1898 how a fishing boat at Peel had always had bad luck, so it was decided to purge it of the buggane (or fairy, or witch) that caused this. A large fire was lit in the ship's hold and was kept going all day until it was judged that the evil spirit had been burned out. At Laxey, meanwhile, the buggane of Lhergy Grawe was laid by burying it beneath the tower of Arnfel House. Across Britain, it is very typical to trap boggarts and the like beneath large stones to imprison them for eternity – compare the treatment meted out to the *buggane* at Chou Traa after it killed Robin's plough horse.[136]

Fynoderee

On the Isle of Man, there are two equivalent beings to the English hobgoblin. The first, the one that most closely resembles its mainland cousin, is the *fynoderee* (a name that can also spelled *fenoderee* and *phynnodderee*). One writer described the being as the "Puck of Manxland" and stressed all its positive qualities: it is "ever present for incitement to agreeable mischief, for actual pitying helpfulness to the weak and for remorseless punishment

---

134 Dora Broome, *Fairy Tales from the Isle of Man*, 1963, 95.
135 *Manx Notes & Queries*, 1904, no.97 and 167-177.
136 *Newcastle Courant*, Nov.28th 1894, 6 'Tales of Ten Travellers;' *Isle of Man Times* May 21st 1895, 4 & June 4th 1892, 2–3.

of the sordid, cruel and the unjust." Another source summarised the *fynoderee* as a "very good sort of spirit" that can even forewarn people of death. It's true that the *fynoderee* is far more benign than the *buggane;* nevertheless, as we shall see, it's not entirely without its faults and dangers.[137]

Fynoderees are known to live on about twelve farms on the island. They don't tend to enter the farmhouses themselves, nor come near to them unless food is left out. They are rarely seen, because during the daytime they keep to caves in the woods and glens. Manx folklorist Mona Douglas described the *fynoderee* in these terms: "he is a faery being who is said to have the body of a goat and the head and shoulders of a man; he may perhaps be called a sort of mythical goat." For this reason, the *fynoderee* has often been compared to a satyr or faun, a reminder of his 'beastly' character. In one account, he is a faery who has been banished from faeryland for courting a human girl and has been transformed in to repulsive form.[138]

The *fynoderee* is a very typical of the semi-domesticated goblin of the British Isles. He is said to part goat with extremely shaggy black hair; some say he's knock-kneed and that his eyes are fiery. He's bigger and broader that a man, very strong but clumsy. Despite his appearance, he can run very quickly and is a tireless and prodigious worker. The *fynoderee* will labour tirelessly threshing a barnful of grain overnight, gathering in hay before a storm or rounding up livestock during a blizzard (in this guise, they're sometimes referred to as 'night men'). What's more, he only asks for a bowl of cream and a handful of scattered grain in recompense.[139]

---

137 *Newcastle Courant,* Nov.28th 1894, 6 'Tales of Ten Travellers;' *Liverpool Mercury,* Sept.9th 1857, 6 'Isle of Man.'
138 Gill, *Manx Scrapbook,* c.4; Douglas, *Forgotten Dances,* 22; *Mona Miscellany* vol.16 1869 173; Jenkinson, *Practical Guide,* 51; Edward Callow, *The Phynnodderee & Other Legends,* 1882.
139 *Mona Miscellany* vol.16 1869 173; Roeder, *Manx Folklore,* 1882; *Manx Notes & Queries,* 1904, no.99; *Manx Notebook,* vol.1, 1885, 'Some Ancient Manx Superstitions.'

At the same time, the *fynoderee*'s also very dim. A man from Maughold once said of the species that "You have to do a bit of the work yourself first, to start it, to show them how like, and then they'd go on with it for you." By way of illustration, one of the species mowed an entire meadow in one night and another whitewashed an entire house overnight. However, the *fynoderee* of Bride parish, working on his own, cut two whole fields of corn in one night and then proceeded to round up the flock of sheep, penning them along with several hares, which he mistook for small, brown and very agile lambs. Likewise, the *fynoderee* of Gordon tried to fetch water in a sieve. Commensurate with his industriousness, the *fynoderee* does not like lazy farmers, so if, for example, the grain is left unthrashed through carelessness and neglect, the *fynoderee* will scatter it in the wind.[140]

Several proofs of the *fynoderee*'s strength are attested. Manx people point to a huge stone that was carried from the beach to a building site by one. In another incident, he met a blacksmith and asked to shake hands. The smith prudently placed a plough share in the *fynoderee*'s grip: it was squeezed just like putty.[141]

The *fynoderee* is friendly towards people, for the most part, but, like many of his kind, he's also very sensitive of criticism and will react violently to perceived slights, stamping a crop flat or mowing so closely behind a farmer who had disparaged his mowing that the man feared having his legs severed, for instance. Like many British hobs, he will also reject human clothes if they're given to him, although in his case it doesn't seem to be principle so much as practicality. For one thing, he is so hairy that garments are

---

[140] Gill, *Third Manx Scrapbook*, c.3; Leney, *Shadowland*, 135; Morrison, *Manx Faery Tales*, 49; Moore, *Folklore*, c.4; *Manx Notes & Queries*, 1904, 99' Gill, *Manx Scrapbook*, c.4, 'Patrick.'

[141] Jenkinson, *Practical Guide*, 91; *Manx Notes & Queries*, 1904, 99; Gill, *Manx Scrapbook*, c.4 'Ballaugh.'

unnecessary in any case; over and above this, clothes can make him ill. In one famous story he expresses his disgust with the gift of suit by complaining:

> "Cap for the head – alas, poor head!
> Coat for the back – alas, poor back!
> Breeches for the breech – alas, poor breech!"

The *fynoderee's* response in this case was to abandon the farm for the solitude of Glen Rushen. This would have been a disaster for the farmer, because it is said that the luck of a house resides in the sprite and, with his departure, all happiness and prosperity will also be gone. Mona Douglas has summarised the *fynoderee's* position as "a being who keeps all the unruly inhabitants of the unseen world in something like order, and holds the human inhabitants of the island under his protection." His presence helps repel the malign influence of witches. Some authorities believe that Manx agriculture as a whole has declined along with the waning belief in – and respect for – the *fynoderee*.[142]

As already suggested, there's a moralistic streak to the *fynoderee*, as with many faery beings. This is very clear in the story of Tholt-e-Will. A farm on Snaefell had been the home of a *fynoderee* for many generations, where it would perform all the farm tasks in return for a sheaf of corn at harvest and a nightly bowl of cream. In due course the farmer died and the property was inherited by Will, who was a spendthrift drunkard. He neglected the land *and* the *fynoderee*. One day a stranger appeared at the farm, offering to buy one of the animals. The offer was rudely rejected by Will, who went on to curse the beast in question. As a result, the animal died, and it seemed that the curse had settled on the entire farm. Will sought

---

[142] Evans Wentz, *Faery Faith*, 129; Douglas, *Forgotten Dances*, 22; Train, *Isle of Man*, vol.2, 138; Harrison, *Mona Miscellany*, 173; Rhys, *Manx Folklore*, Part One; *Manx Notes & Queries*, 1904, 99; Gill, *Manx Scrapbook*, 1929, c.4.

the advice of a local witch on lifting the malediction, but instead he fell into the power of her coven and was carried off by a *glashtyn*.[143]

The *fynoderee* also seems to be able to influence human welfare and wealth more generally. There was one that lived amongst the gorse and oak trees growing around Scroundal Mill. Eventually these shrubs were cleared and the man who did the work was ill for a long time afterwards. Like all faery beings, it is clearly not wise to anger or upset the *fynoderee*. Bear in mind, too, that they can be subdued by singing, but driven off by the singing of hymns.[144]

Conversely, the *fynoderee* may indulge in acts of spontaneous charity. At Struan y Granghee, near Laxey, a hermit lived alone in a cave. He'd been cheated on by his girl, had fought his rival in love and killed him, so he had gone to live alone. The local *fynoderee* took pity on the man and looked after him, bringing him food and firewood on winter. As the hermit got older, the *fynoderee* planted oaks near to his cave so there was wood readily accessible.[145]

Lastly, in one story the *fynoderee* is depicted as a solitary creature living in elder trees. He has the power to cure sickness in animals, and can be summoned by humans using the right words and charms. The correct protocol is to take off your headgear and say to the being in the tree:

> "Fynoderee, fynoderee,
> Come you down, for I can see."

Then you must cross yourself three times. Getting the words wrong or neglecting to cross yourself can lead to disastrous consequences – in this instance, the fynoderee stole away the farm's entire livestock.[146]

---

143 *Isle of Man Times,* October 1st 1898, 2 'A Scrap of Manx Folklore.'
144 Gill, *Manx Scrapbook,* c.4 'Ballaugh.'
145 *Mannin,* vol.1, 'A Manx Notebook;' Broome, *Fairy Tales,* c.16.
146 Broome, *Fairy Tales,* c.4.

Glashtyn

The second Manx hob is called the *glashan*, *glastin* or *glashtyn*. As we have already seen, this being has one form as a water horse, but it may also be encountered as a lamb playing amongst a flock of sheep, a pig and even as a water bull or *tarroo ushtey*. However, he will mostly be seen as a large hairy naked man (though female *glashtyns* are also known), who is simple and coarse and prone to grudges. An example of their stupidity is the regular story of a *glashtyn* herding in the flock of sheep with which he has also – with very great trouble – rounded up a hare.[147]

There are two separate types of *glashtyn*, although both beings are like naked men, large and powerful, with shaggy dark hair and pale complexions. The first is semi-domesticated, living in pools in rivers near to the farms where it works. These *glashtyns* are good-natured and helpful to those whom they favour. They can be like faithful dogs, following farmers around, and they are stupid, clumsy and can take offence very easily. Because of their strength, they are able to thresh a whole stack of corn in a single night, and will also tend grain drying in kilns overnight. In return for their labours, people would bank up the cottage fire for them to enjoy at night but would never speak to them. The semi-domesticated *glashtyn* like so many of his kind, doesn't like to be given clothes and doesn't like to be overseen. One on a farm at Bradda that was engaged in drying grain realised that a man was spying on him and he snatched up the offender and threw him into the hot kiln as well. Fortunately some kindly faeries intervened and pulled the victim out.[148]

---

147 Roeder, *Manx Folktales,* 26; Moore, *Folklore,* c.4.
148 *Yn Lioar Manninagh,* vol.III; Roeder, *Manx Folktales,* 26; *Manx Notes & Queries,* 1904, no.98; Gill, *Manx Scrapbook,* c.4; Moore, *Folklore,* c.4.

The second type of *glashtyn* is savage and wild-roaming, living on moorland in marshes, behind waterfalls or in deep pools in isolated rivers. The Isle of Man used to be infested with them. This variety has very unpleasant habits, such as trying to drag women into pools by seizing their skirts with their teeth. The *glashtyn* at Braddan haunted the church-yard there and was described as being short and hairy with an evil face. If you wanted to pass the spot, you had to bow three times to appease him.[149]

In the shape of a handsome (if rather hairy) young man, the wild *glashtyn* will try to lure away young women with strings of pearls, but his intentions are not romantic but fatal. His true nature is often revealed by his pointed ears and his sharp, pointed teeth. One in horse form was revealed by his tail, which was three yards long.[150]

These creatures were, as a class, seen as malevolent and terrifying. This is confirmed by a rhyme from the Isle of Man in which an unfaithful lover is cursed, successively, with injury from the water bull, the night steed, the 'rough satyr' (that is, the *glashtyn*) the faery of the glen (*ferrish ny glionney*) and with bogles. Pity the two-timing partner who faces this supernatural assault.[151]

Because of their predatory nature, *glashtyns* can be a severe nuisance that communities need to expel. In one story this was done by a man disguising himself as a woman and sitting spinning in his home until a number of young *glashtins* had gathered, interested in this new girl in the neighbourhood. He then surprised them by pelting them with burning turves, a shock that was sufficient to drive them off permanently. Finally, the trick of aiming to strike a blow, and then pulling it back, is as effective with *glashtyns* as it is with a tarroo ushtey. It renders the creature powerless to retaliate.[152]

---

149 Gill, *Manx Scrapbook*, c.4; Moore, *Folklore*, c.4; *Manx Notes & Queries*, 98.
150 Broome, *Fairy Tales*, c.8; *Yn Lioar Manninagh*, vol.2, 194–7.
151 Harrison, *Mona Miscellany*, 65.
152 *Mona Miscellany*, 2nd series, 21, 1873, 248; *Yn Lioar Manninagh*, vol.III.

Faery Beasts

The *glashtyn* described in the last chapter can take horse form; the water bull and the water horse have the shape of the conventional animals, but their habitats and behaviour can be noticeably different. There are, in addition to these, a number of supernatural animals on the Isle of Man that much more closely resemble the normal beasts, but have some unusual qualities or powers. Apparently, fairy animals often wear red or blue caps, just like the fairies themselves. This is, plainly, a very easy way of identifying them as being different to the ordinary human pet or farm beast.[153]

Faery Horses

As well as the water horse described before, there's also a second fae horse on the island, which is called the *cabbyl ny hole, cabbyl oie* or 'night horse', who appears to be of largely benign disposition. It may possibly just be another manifestation of the *cabbyl ushtey*. The night horse roams the roads of the island after dark in the form of a grey colt or horse that is ready saddled and bridled. It will willingly carry travellers who are out late home to their doors. However, if the horse takes a dislike to the person it's carrying, it may gallop along at a terrifying pace before tossing them off or even carrying them away into a river or the sea (unless they've protected themselves with a blessing). As an example of this mistreament, a man out on

---

153 Gill, *Second Manx Scrapbook,* c.6.

a cold morning saw a saddled horse standing alone and decided to mount it. It immediately plunged into a pool with its victim on its back. Then it surfaced, dropped him on the bank, and sank beneath the surface again. The night horse seems to like to give shocks, therefore, but no more. This contrasts to the *glashan/ glashtyn*, which represents a far more deadly risk to unwary travellers.[154]

There is also a possible third type of faery horse, called by some the 'spirit horse.' Galloping hooves have frequently been heard across the island, without there being any horses in the vicinity who might have produced the sound and without any marks being left on the ground. Other witnesses have seen a white horse, often high on the mountains, and some strange hooved tracks have also been found. Ghostly horses and carriages, sometimes with child-sized women riding inside, have also been reported.[155]

What presumably is another manifestation of the *cabbyl ny hole* has been reported. If you step inadvertently on the herb called belly-wort, a fairy horse will appear and carry you around all night against your will. In another version of this lore, it's said that to step on St John's Wort on St John's Eve will conjure up the fae horse.[156]

A fairy donkey, which turned into a huge black dog, was seen once near the foot of Snaefell. Lastly, mention must be made of the horses the fairies ride for their hunts. These look like the steeds kept by humans, except for the necessary fact that they are never bigger than a foal. They are, as is often the way with such beasts, white with red ears.[157]

---

154 Roeder, *Manx Folklore*, 1882–85; *Yn Lioar Manninagh*, vol.1, part 2, 291.
155 Gill, *Manx Scrapbook*, c.4; Moore, *Folklore*, c.4; Roeder, *Manx Folktales*, 22; Train, *Isle of Man*, vol.2, c.18; Gill, *Third Manx Scrapbook*, Part 2, c.3; *Yn Lioar Manninagh*, vol.III 485; *Manx Notes & Queries*, 1904, no.93 & 139–140; Roeder, *Manx Folklore*, 1882–85.
156 Gill, *Second Manx Scrapbook*, c.6; Moore, *Folklore*, c.7.
157 Gill, *Third Manx Scrapbook*, Part 2, c.3; Douglas, *Forgotten Dances*, 19.

Faery Pig

The faery pig of the Isle of Man is called *arkan sonney* in Manx – 'the lucky piggy'. It is a white pig with red ears and eyes that is capable of changing its size, but which can't change its shape. They are very attractive creatures and having one amongst your swine herd will bring you luck. If a fisherman sees the pig at the start of the fishing season, he will enjoy good catches that year. The *arkan sonney* is most often seen by children at dusk in the Patrick area of Man; the important thing, once you've spotted the pig, is not to take your off it. If you do, it will vanish. Another pig is said to appear around Glenfaba and wears a red hat. All the Manx pigs are said to have considerable magical powers.[158]

Simply seeing the pig can bring good luck, as happened to one woman who came across it running along at night. She did not try to catch or touch it, and for a period of time after that she would find silver coins in her pockets whenever she put in her hand in need of change. Eventually, as often happens in these cases, she told a friend of her good fortune – and lost the fairy gift. Conversely, a young man who followed the fairy pig was struck down with a sharp pain in his leg which could only be healed by a magical intervention.[159]

The faeries of the Isle of Man also keep livestock in the normal course of their farming. The pigs raised by the faery farmers are identifiable by the fact that they're white with a feathery tail rather like a fan, long, loppy ears and burning red eyes.

---

158 See my *Faeries* chapter 5; Douglas, *Forgotten Dances*, 21–22; Morrison, *Manx Fairy Tales*, 100; Broome, *Fairy Tales*, 46–52; Cashen, c.2.
159 *Manx Notes & Queries*, 1904, 153; Morrison, *Manx Fairy Tales*, 100.

Faery Sheep

Faery lambs are generally very appealing. Their fleeces are bright red (though some are apparently white but wear a scarlet jacket). Sometimes one will appear in a farm's flock and when they do so they bring good luck, increasing the health and fertility of the normal sheep. A woman at Malew saw a lamb in her flock in a red saddle and bridle. She tried to touch it, but it instantly vanished. Afterwards, she realised that this had probably been a lucky escape, as she suspected that contact with the creature would have paralysed her.[160]

As mentioned with pigs, the fairies will raise their own livestock for food. It seems that the little people often expand their flocks by stealing sheep from humans. To do this, they use their glamour to make it impossible for a shepherd to accurately count the sheep he's tending. The only remedy is to wash his eyes in running water first. The explanation for this apparently unrelated cure seems to be the fact that the Little People, like most British faeries, cannot cross running streams.[161]

Finally, there are reports of a creature called the *ghoayr haddagh* (the antic goat), which may be heard bleating on calm nights. Its voice resembles that of a goat, but much louder and sounding like laughter – although most people are terrified by hearing it. It seems to live in bogs and marshy places and scares people passing with its strange bleating. In one of her stories, Dora Broome described an eerie goat that dances with the fairies and has some strange affinity with them.[162]

---

160 Gill, *Second Manx Scrapbook*, c.6.
161 Douglas, *Forgotten Dances*, 21; *Yn Lioar Manninagh*, vol.1, part 2, 290.
162 *Manx Notes & Queries*, 1904, 167; Broome, *More Fairy Tales*, c.4.

Faery Cattle

Manx faery cows are said to be red-eared, like their Scottish and Irish relatives. There is also reported to be a black faery calf that is headless (or has a jangling chain around its neck) which brings bad luck to those who meet it. Only a few encounters with the beast are recorded. In the lower part of Glen Maye a girl saw it hanging about a gateway on dark evening. It didn't approach her, but jumped across the lane into a deep place below the waterfall, making a rattling noise; nevertheless, she was never well again in consequence of the fright she got. Another girl saw one at the Folly, between Castletown and Ballasalla, a spot where many other strange things have been seen and heard.[163]

Faery Hounds

Like the British mainland, the Isle of Man has its own supernatural black dogs and these alarming apparitions continued to be seen well into the twentieth century. These creatures are called the *moddey dhoo*, which is merely Manx for 'black dog.' The *moddey* has been described as "a large black spaniel with curly hair," which doesn't make it sound too bad at all; at the other extreme it's been labelled the "black dog of death," whilst folklorist Mona Douglas opted for a middle course, saying that it had a "bad reputation" and, even in 1970, was still feared on the island, although it would generally not molest people if they didn't molest it. The best advice upon meeting one plainly is to exercise great caution.[164]

---

163 Gill, *Second Manx Scrapbook,* c.6; see too Broome, *Fairy Tales,* c.19.
164 *Aberdeen Journal,* Sept.11th, 1886, 3 'Manx Bogies;' *Newcastle Courant,* Nov.28th 1894, 6 'Tales of Ten Travellers;' Mona Douglas, 'Secret Land of Legends,' *The Times,* Jan.2nd 1970, 27.

The *moddey dhoo* is widespread across the island, haunting roads and lanes mostly (though the one at Ballahutchin lived in a barn), and sometimes appearing headless (as, for example, at Kinlye's Glen, Milntown, Ballaugh Glen, Mooragh, Dreamskerry, Dhoon and Hango). They will howl, scream and chase people. The most famous example was known at Peel Castle in the seventeenth century. It used to appear at night and lie in the guardroom. The troops of the garrison eventually got used to its company, although even so they would never swear in its presence nor were any of them ever prepared to be left alone with the hound. Other Manx examples are agreed to be very large ("half the size of a calf" in one report), shaggy and black with fiery, saucer eyes. They tend to haunt particular locations, where they will prowl up and down. They cannot be heard either breathing or walking, but from time to time their howls will be heard in the distance. Besides terrifying people and horses, and occasionally pulling riders from their mounts, these hounds do not seem to do any great harm unless they are molested. Their howls are sometimes regarded as forecasts of calamity. The *moddey dhoo* of Lezayre, for example, was seen a few nights before a torrential downpour that led to disastrous floods in Glen Auldyn.[165]

Like other nuisance faery beings such as *bugganes*, the *moddey dhoo* sometimes has to be laid, or exorcised. In one case, at Dreamskerry, this was done in traditional religious manner with prayers and exhortations. In another case, at Ballaugh Glen, a man's bold (or foolhardy) attempt to grab the hound appears to have been enough to banish it permanently. Perhaps this may be compared to the *tarroo ushtey* at Ramsey that was tamed by threatening to strike it.[166]

As well as the *moddey dhoo*, there are more conventional looking dogs kept by the faeries, and that partake of some of their owner's

---

165 Gill, *Manx Scrapbook*, c.4 & *Third Manx Scrapbook*, c.3; Waldron, *Isle of Man*, 23; Douglas, *Forgotten Dances*, 16–17.
166 Gill, *Third Manx Scrapbook*, Part 2, c.3.

supernatural qualities. There is a Manx saying, "a dog that has a fairy eye" which seems to imply something distinctive about the eyes of faery hounds, just like their owners.[167]

Although by no means as large or as threatening as the *moddey dhoo*, it can still be unpleasant to encounter the faery hounds. A man, who was carrying some fresh fish, was followed home one evening by a pack of fairy dogs. When he arrived at his own door, he picked up a stone and threw it among them, whereupon they disappeared. He paid for his rashness, though, being ill for six months afterwards. Neighbours advised him that he would have been left alone if only he had put a pinch of salt in the fishes' mouths, as the fairies couldn't stand it. As will be seen in the next chapter, this remedy will protect a person from faeries as well as from their hounds.[168]

Another man encountered a crowd of fairy dogs covering the road in Arbory one night. He could tell that they weren't ordinary hounds because they were so small and black. He invoked a holy name and the dogs promptly vanished. A man at nearby Cregneash was once surrounded by hundreds of tiny dogs when he was out walking and another man from near Spanish Head found himself surrounded by the faery hunt's pack of hounds: he heard whistling and soon had twenty dogs and then the hunters coursing past him. In a fourth incident, a man came upon a large number of hounds filling the road one night; he waited for a very long time for them to pass and became extremely impatient. Although there was no contact with them, it seems that his bad temper rebounded upon him, and he was ill for a long period afterwards.[169]

Faery hounds aren't always large and scary. In about 1898 two men were in a small boat fishing round the Calf, when they saw a

---

167 Gill, *Manx Scrapbook*, c.4, 'Patrick.'
168 Moore, *Folklore*, c.3; Rhys, *Manx Folklore*, Part One.
169 *Yn Lioar Manninagh*, vol.II, 194–7 & vol.III; *Manx Notes & Queries*, 1904, 181 & 178.

pretty little dog upon a rock near the water. They rowed to rescue it and one went on shore, but when he was just in the act of taking hold of the dog it vanished in a flash of fire, and both of the men were sick after for a long time.[170]

Finally, there is another Manx faery dog, called the *coo ny helg* (the hunting dog) which is to be seen running in fields, or even on the road, in the evening. It is white with red ears or feet and, if you see it and say '*Shee dy row adhene*' ('bless the faeries') you will be endowed with good luck.[171]

Faery Cats

There are two reports of very alarming fairy cats. One night, a man was about to shut and lock his cottage door when he saw a white cat sitting just outside. He went to shoo it away, but it would not move. He then, unwisely, tried to kick it, in response to which it stood up and then swelled up to an enormous size, almost blocking out the sky. Fortunately, it then walked away, leaving the cottager understandably terrified. In a related incident, a man from Fistard was walking home when he saw a black cat, which again he tried to kick. His foot met with nothing and the cat swelled up and turned into a black bull with huge horns. It blocked his path and drove him out of the field, over the stile and to a nearby house where he took shelter. This may have been a *buggane* in one of his many forms.[172]

Nowhere near as threatening, but just as unsettling, was the experience of another man who had to walk home from the Howe several nights in a row. Each time, he found himself accompanied by a mysterious black cat which vanished when he approached it.[173]

---

170 *Manx Notes & Queries*, 1904, 179
171 Douglas, *Forgotten Dances*, 17.
172 *Mannin*, no.7, 1916; *Manx Notes & Queries*, 1904, 20.
173 *Manx Notes & Queries*, 1904, 182.

Human Relations

The relationship between the Manx islanders and the isle's faery population has always been fraught. As a result, the fairies are blamed by people for all the misfortunes they suffer – for falling down or tripping, for items that go missing and such like. That said, interactions are not uniformly bad. George Waldron, for example, said that people often saw the fairies and were not afraid of them because they knew that they brought good luck.[174]

Certain people are able to see the faeries because they have received the second sight, often by stepping on a magical spot or by treading on certain herbs. Adopting the right posture or gesture, or "thinking of nothing" may also work. Dogs naturally possess the second sight and can see fairies; regrettably, they are afraid of them. Cats, by contrast, are on good terms with the Little People: when fairies visit a home at night, only the *pussy boght* is permitted to stay in the kitchen when the rest of the household have retired to bed. Horses too can detect supernaturals, and are terrified of them – to the extent that they may even drop dead from fear. An illustration of this comes from Orry's Dale. Here, there was once no bread delivery because the baker's boy said that his cart horse was able to see the fairies after dark and would take fright. On this particular occasion, as it was getting near dusk the

---

[174] *Mona Miscellany* vol.16 1869 173; Jenkinson, *Practical Guide,* 38; Waldron, *Isle of Man,* 27 & 65.

boy decided not to risk the horse rearing or bolting – and had gone home instead.[175]

Some people are on very good terms with the fairies – for example, Walter Gill describes a man near to whose house was a pool where the fairies used to congregate. He would go and sit by the pool and debate with them on politics and other matters, although the risk was that if he disagreed with them too forcefully, they would simply throw him into the water. However, at a hedge (dry stone wall) on his own farm about a quarter of a mile away a Scottish man frequently spoke with the red-hatted Manx fairies, and one day his shepherd found him lying there, dead.[176]

Having a good relationship with the *ferrishyn* might be materially beneficial. For example, author Dora Broome described how the fairies could affect the prices at markets, making them go up and down as they chose to assist a favoured human.[177]

Faery Rules

The moral code imposed by *bugganes* and *fynoderees* has already been mentioned. Like all faery populations in Britain, the Manx faeries have a set of rules with which they expect the humans living beside them to respect. These principles are never set out clearly to us, however, and we must work out what's acceptable and what's *taboo* by trial and error, by reward and bitter experience. Nevertheless, some rules are pretty obvious: for example, it is *never* advisable at all to break a promise made to a fairy.[178]

---

175 Gill, *Second Manx Scrapbook*, c.6; Douglas, *Forgotten Dances*, 17; Gill, *Third Manx Scrapbook*, Part 2, c.3; *Yn Lioar Manninagh*, vol.III, 482.
176 Gill, *Second Manx Scrapbook*, c.6.
177 Broome, *Fairy Tales*, 11.
178 Broome, *Fairy Tales*, 12.

HUMAN RELATIONS

Other tenets of the faery moral code are less predictable, but island folk have learned them over the centuries. The faeries object to baking after sunset, but otherwise they will help with bread making so long as a piece of the dough is stuck to the kitchen wall as an offering. If such a gift isn't made, the baker will face problems.[179]

In addition, it's very important to remember that the faeries don't like salt in their loaves. A woman was out walking when she heard music ahead of her on the road. She followed the sound and caught up with a group of fairies. They asked what she had in her basket, to which she replied bread, offering to share it with them. She broke one of the oatcakes she had with her and placed it on a hedge. They accepted her offer after checking that there was no salt in the mix. Because of her generosity, she was promised always to have bread. As this account indicates, the faeries expect, even require, that humans will share their stocks of food with them. So, for example, the common practice was to leave the last cake of a batch behind the 'turf-flag' for the little people; another account describes a woman living by the mouth of Ballaugh River who was baking bonnags, when a little child appeared, to whom she gave a bonnag. As soon as it touched her hand, the child disappeared. It's advisable to put out spoons under the table at meal times so that the faeries can help themselves to a share of your repast. Similarly, harvest meals should be shared with the fairies, with a little bread and butter being set to one side for them by the workers in the fields. In one case at Glen Maye, this wasn't done and a very small woman suddenly appeared and made loud complaint, until a share was given her. A second account concerns a girl baking at Bride. She forgot the custom of sharing the resulting oat cake with the fairies but, when she went up to sleep and got into bed, she received

---

[179] A. Moore, *Folklore of the Isle of Man* (London, Nutt, 1891) c.3; Train, *Isle of Man*, vol.2, c.XVIII; Morrison, *Manx Fairy Tales*, 10.

a blow to her face. Knowing this to be a message from the aggrieved little people, she went straight back down, baked a new cake and left it out for the *ferrishyn*.[180]

The little people are also very particular about peace and quiet and respect for undisturbed enjoyment of their homes. So, when the flour mill was built at Colby, the local faeries abandoned their former haunts: early one morning they were seen climbing up into the mists and solitude of the mountain glens, making a "low, pathetic, forlorn moaning" and with all their household goods on their backs, including spinning wheels, kettles, pots and pans. Waldron told a similar story of a fairy flight from a newly opened fulling mill at Beary, when multitudes were seen, crossing the river on stepping stones and likewise burdened. They were said to be dressed in pointed red caps and clothes made of the dark brown wool of the Manx *loaghtyn* sheep. Likewise, the arrival of the railways and other trappings of modern technology and industry have been very distressing to them. Describing the Isle of Man in 1874, Henry Irwin Jenkinson worried that the advent of railways and tourists (and, for that matter, Primitive Methodist chapels) meant that "the last haunts of the good people will be invaded and they will have to move elsewhere."[181]

Protections Against Faeries

It was well-known what harm the fairies could do, as reflected in the following curse:

---

180 *Proceedings of the Isle of Man Natural History & Archaeological Society*, vol.1, Jan.1889; *Yn Lioar Manninagh*, vol.1 223 & III; Roeder, *Manx Folk Tales*, 14; *Yn Lioar Manninagh*, vol.II, 194–7.
181 A. Herbert, *The Isle of Man*, 1909, 177; Waldron, *Isle of Man*, fn.46; Jenkinson, *Practical Guide*, London: E. Stanford,1874, 75 & 106.

"What if the spotted water-bull,
And the Glashtyn were to take you,
And the Fynoderee of the glen, waddling,
To make of you a bolster against the wall.

The Fairy of the Glen and the Buggane?...
May they gather together about your bed,
And in a straw-rope creel run off with you."[182]

Over the generations, the Manx population has developed a battery of protections and remedies for dealing with the potential faery threat. There are, fortunately, a wide range of substances and techniques that will ward off or repel supernatural harm.

Some of the protections are extremely simple, the defensive powers of simple hedgerow flowers being a very good example of this. The mugwort (*bolugh* or *bollian-feaill-eoin*), with its creamy-white blossoms, protects from faery harm, so Manx farmers have long garlanded themselves and their cattle with these flowers at Midsummer. Four leafed clover is equally efficacious, as is vervain, sprigs of which were sometimes sown into clothes to provide perpetual protection to wearers, usually vulnerable ones such as children.[183]

Homes are protected from faery intrusions with yellow flowers on Midsummer's Eve. Gorse flowers are yellow and this – coupled with its spikes – may be the reason the bush is so effective as a barrier against fays. Gorse (*koinney*) was also set alight on May Eve to drive the faeries away from the fields. All the same, the primary protective plant is the (yellow) St John's Wort, which is hung around houses on Midsummer's Eve (St John's Eve). Ragwort (*cushag*) and

---

182 Morrison, *Manx Folk Tales,* 143; 'The Song of the Fairies,' Gill, *Second Manx Scrapbook,* c.8.
183 Moore, *Folklore,* c.7; Broome, *More Fairy Tales,* 40; *Yn Lioar Manninagh* vol.1, part 2, 289.

primrose are also recommended: children would pick the latter and scatter it before doors on May Eve to keep the Little Folk out. These facts notwithstanding, folk beliefs often prove contradictory. It's also said that if you pick the St John's Wort after sunset on Midsummer's Eve, a faery horse will appear and carry you away. This festival used to be particularly significant on the Isle of Man; in addition to wearing certain plants and flowers, protective fires were lit to safeguard people and livestock from the island fays.[184]

Another useful plant is the stinging nettle. Fresh nettles will stop the faeries hindering the churning of butter; you must first beat the churn with the plants and then lay them on top of it. Two common shrubs can help safeguard against the *ferrishyn* too, as we have already seen. The rowan or mountain ash is held in esteem throughout the British Isles for its ability to repel supernatural threats. The leaves or twigs are effective in themselves, but if they're shaped in to the form of a Christian cross, they are even more beneficial. Equally, whilst the faeries like elder bushes, carrying a few of the shrub's leaves can repel them.[185]

As we shall see again later, iron and steel, in the form of any kind of tool or household implement, are extremely effective in keeping faery threats at bay. A Manx man found himself surrounded one night by a herd of vicious faery steeds; he was able to fend them off for hours with his knife until dawn came and they vanished.[186]

I have already mentioned the fact that salt is another readily available and highly protective substance. It's scattered under the door to protect a house, a custom known as *queeltah*. Salt thrown in a churn will avoid any faery interference with the butter making process. Likewise, the Manx belief is that, if you're carrying milk

---

184 Gill, *Second Manx Scrapbook*, c.6; Moore, *Folklore*, c.3; Herbert, *Isle of Man*, 176; E. Hull, *Folklore of the British Isles*, 251.
185 *Yn Lioar Manninagh*, vol.4, 35; Harrison, *Mona Miscellany*, 140.
186 *Yn Lioar Manninagh* vol.3.

in a pail, you should add a small pinch of salt to it, which will ensure that the fairies don't steal or spoil the contents during the journey. Perhaps this information explains the recollection of an elderly woman in late Victorian times that she used to see the fairies playing in the trees around her home when she was little; one time, when the girl was carrying a milk pail, they had pinched her severely. This an interesting conclusion to her anecdote, as she had started by describing the fairies as tiny, winged and dancing on sunbeams: "the good people from sunset land." Evidently, they weren't as harmless as she had initially supposed.[187]

A very curious example of the protective property of salt was reported in the early 1880s. A woman had killed and butchered one of her calves and decided to send her son with a cut of the meat as a gift to a poor neighbour. In her hurry, however, the mother forgot to protect the joint by sprinkling salt on it. As the boy walked over to the friend's house, the local fairies realised that the meat was vulnerable and they followed the youth – licking him until he was sore over his entire body. When he got home, his mother had to wash him all over in salt in order to dispel the fairies' magic. It's a little hard to explain exactly what happened here: perhaps in licking the 'goodness' out of the meat the fairies also touched the boy's bare arms, legs and face, thereby subjecting him to their power with their spit. The protective power of salt is clear, nonetheless.[188]

Carrying salt in your pocket is a good protection when you're out and about or on a journey. It's also strewed about a house before a woman gives birth and a little is put in the newborn's mouth. For the same reasons, it is sprinkled lightly over provisions, over farm implements and sea tackle, particularly the nets.[189]

---

187 *Yn Lioar Manninagh* vol.1, part 2, 289; Cumming, *Guide to the Isle of Man*, 22; *Mannin*, no.1, 1913, 'Folklore Notes;' Roeder, *Manx Folktales*, 19.
188 Roeder, *Manx Folklore*, 1882–85.
189 Gill, *Second Manx Scrapbook,* cc.4 & 6; Moore, *Folklore*, c.7.

A number of animal products also have a prophylactic quality. On St Catherine's Day (November 25th) a black hen would be killed and its blood would be sprinkled on the threshold of the house and the byre and stable if needs be. The hen was then carried sunwise around the house before being buried on its east side. Long ago, the Manx population discovered that two animal bones have a powerful protective effect. These were the *crosh bollan,* which is the upper part of the palate of the wrass fish, and the so-called *Thor's Hammer,* which is in fact from a sheep's mouth and prevents fairy leading.[190]

Stale urine, which is collected to use in clothes washing, is objectionable to the Little People, as has already been mentioned. Another use of the liquid is to protect ploughs from fairy influence: the practice has been to throw it over the implement to prevent interference in the farming process.[191]

Spells, charms and other forms of words can keep the faery threat at bay. The *Mona Miscellany* of 1873 records an incantation that was to be said at night to protect a home from fairy incursions:

> "The peace of God and the peace of man,
> The peace of God and Columb Killey,
> On each window and each door,
> And on every hole admitting moonlight,
> And on the place of my rest
> And the peace of God on myself."[192]

One thing to bear in mind with all of magical forms of words is the need to repeat them exactly as they have been formulated. We

---

[190] Douglas, *Forgotten Dances,* 10; *Mannin,* no.3, 1913, 2; Dora Broome, *Fairy Tales,* 76–79 & 95.
[191] *Yn Lioar Manninagh* vol.1, part 2, 289.
[192] *Mona Miscellany,* 2nd series, vol.21, 1873, 195; Harrison, *Mona Miscellany,* 193; Morrison, *Manx Fairy Tales,* 186.

saw in earlier how errors in reciting charms to a mermaid and a *fynoderee* can have exactly opposite effects to those intended.

It is widely understood that there is an antipathy between the faeries and the rituals, signs and structures of the Christian church. This being so, a simple blessing will almost always suffice to dispel faery harm. A small woman in a red cloak carrying a can suddenly appeared in front of boy working cutting peats in a bog on Snaefell. Guessing she was a faery, he immediately crossed himself and said a charm. She vanished with a howl.[193]

Effective as Christian invocations are, the problem is that they have become ingrained in everyday speech as exclamations used without any explicit religious purpose. This fact can cause considerable inconvenience from time to time. A man was familiar with the fairies and used to meet with them regularly. They would ride through the sky, the fairies on their horses and the man on the beam of his loom. Unfortunately, when they reached a point where the ground fell way sharply beneath him, he instinctively blessed himself and, instantly, the party vanished and the weaver sank to the ground, and had to walk all the way home carrying the heavy loom beam on his shoulder.[194]

As I mentioned a little earlier, the *ferrishyn* object to loud noises. As a result, firing guns and blowing horns was used for many years on Man to try to drive away the ever-present threat of the fairies and evil spirits. As specific examples of this practice, on the morning of a wedding, it was a custom for young men to climb the highest neighbouring hill, there to blow cow-horns as long as their breath held out. The intention was to ward off the fairies, and for the same reason the same music was performed on the morning of the May 12th (Old May Day), to prevent the fairies stealing children.[195]

---

193 *Mannin*, no.7, 1916; Douglas, *Forgotten Dances*, 1.
194 *Yn Lioar Manninagh*, III.
195 Harrison, *Mona Miscellany*, 193; Gill, *Second Manx Scrapbook*, c.4.

Faeries in Human Homes

The Manx *ferrishyn* seem to treat human houses with great familiarity. As it's believed that the fairies avoid human wickedness and towns, where that sinfulness is most concentrated, it's regarded as a mark of blessing if they favour an individual's house. Hence, it's said that they never come without bringing good fortune with them.

The faeries will enter at night, build up the fires and make use of the spinning wheels or the butter churns. Because of their magical abilities, it's impossible to exclude them or lock them out: "no bolts or bars will keep them out," so that it was customary for people to leave their doors open at night. In addition, the visitors expect bread and water to be left out for them (although, of course, the fairies were very likely to steal the food they fancied anyway, if it wasn't provided voluntarily). Furthermore, it was accepted that on dark and stormy nights the little folk would need to be able to shelter somewhere, so people would bank up their fires and go to bed early to make way for them. This habit was called the 'fairies' welcome' or *shee dy vea*. In the *Fairy Faith in Celtic Countries*, Evans Wentz recorded a witness saying that his grandfather's family would sometimes be visited by a little white dog on cold winter's nights. This was a fairy dog, and it was a sign that the fairies themselves were on their way. The family would then stop whatever they were doing and make the house ready (fire stoked and fresh water set out) before hurrying off to bed.[196]

The faeries are particularly insistent that water must be set out in bowls every night for them; some households also put out oatcakes. This water should never be used by the household in the morning,

---

196 Roeder, *Manx Folktales*, 1; Moore, *Folklore*, c.3; Broome, *Fairy Tales*, 40; Wentz, 122 & 132; Cumming, *Guide*, 23; Gill, *Third Manx Scrapbook*, Part 2, c.3; Broome, *More Fairy Tales*, 24–25.

but should be thrown away. Woe betide any maid or householder who overlooks this duty before going to bed. The least that will happen is that the fairies will disturb the peoples' sleep; if they're wise, they will then get up and correct their oversight – after which they will sleep soundly, but in one case the neglectful servant was struck by the fairies and her mouth was left crooked for the rest of her life. As we shall see later, part of the reason that water was left out overnight was not so much courtesy to the *ferrishyn*, but to ensure that the little people had something available to quench their thirsts – otherwise they might take some of the sleepers' blood.[197]

As we saw in the previous section, faery-kind are averse to iron. It is therefore only common courtesy to ensure that all metal implements such as pokers have been put away at night before they arrive. Interestingly, though, at Easter the custom was to replace the iron poker with a rowan wood one, specifically to repel the fairies.[198]

On Halloween in particular it was expected that the fairies would enter homes, often with more malign intent than usual. In order to protect the household against any harm, people would go to bed leaving out not just fresh water, milk or cream but all the food uneaten at the end of their evening meal.[199]

The fairies often enter homes to dance and they have been heard playing their music in a house kitchen at Ballakillowey and singing in a garden at Castle Mona. Conversely, though, it has been alleged that their presence near a house was a sign of impending trouble or death.[200]

The honest truth is that the faeries do pretty much what they want in human homes, as the following accounts indicate. There

---

197 *Mona Miscellany*, 2nd series, 21, 1873, 194; Harrison, *Mona Miscellany*, 193; Jenkinson, *Practical Guide*, 75; *Yn Lioar Manninagh*, III.
198 *Mannin*, no.3, 1913; Herbert. *Isle of Man*, 217.
199 Leney, *Shadowland in Ellan Vannin*, 146.
200 Gill, *Manx Scrapbook*, c.4 'Ballaugh.'; *Second Manx Scrapbook*, c.6.

was once a house in Glenchass, which had a reputation for being haunted. The man who lived there was woken one night by a great noise in the kitchen. He got out of bed and discovered a great many people in the room, and a great number of candles burning. The faeries had set up a long bench with a fine joint of beef laid upon it and they were busy carving the meat up, chopping with cleavers and cutting with saws. The man didn't say a word, but got into bed again. He was expecting in the morning to find all the furniture smashed, but everything was as he had left it and all the beef had been taken away, leaving not even a stain of blood nor trace of their butchering to be seen.[201]

A man who lived in the cottage on Mull Hill often had the fairies entering his home when he and his wife were in bed. The fairies were very small and they would play, jump and dance about the room; however, they said very little to each other if they sensed that the humans were not yet asleep. The man was awake one night when the fairy visitors arrived, and this time they were accompanied by a much larger individual. He approached the couple's bed, so the man closed his eyes and pretended to be asleep. The fairy bent over him and then he said to the rest in Manx "*Ta'n ghenn chellagh ny ehadley er aght erbee*" ('the old cock is asleep anyway'). Another man, living in a house not far from the Chasms, had to put up with the fairies coming inside his home every evening about sunset, even when he and his wife were still sitting by the fire. He reported that these visitors looked like little boys about seven years of age, and wore leather caps. They would come and go freely and sometimes would venture quite near to the couple at the fire, but they never did any mischief, so he never molested them, but rather let them dance and jump as much as they pleased. In another account, the fairies even seemed to be undertaking building work on the human's cow house,

---

[201] *Manx Notes & Queries,* 1904, 119.

because there was a sound like the thudding of sledge hammers against the wall.[202]

As this last example suggests, the faeries will use human buildings for work as well as for pleasure. Several Manx tales warn how a failure to disengage the drive band on a spinning wheel before retiring to bed enables the faeries to come into a house overnight to use it for their own purposes.[203] In this connection, it's worth remarking upon the strong views the fairies seem to hold about *when* it is appropriate for people to make thread. Evenings and Saturdays are particularly prohibited. This may be evidence of some wider aversion, as baking in the evenings is also abhorred, or it may be something to do with their own wish to use the equipment.[204]

The fairies are also known to enter mills at night and grind their own corn there. The mill at Scroundal was a particular haunt. Apparently, they used to sit on the grind stone of the mill when it was in use and sing with happiness as it turned, holding lights in their hands.[205]

Faery Thefts

The fairies consider that they are entitled by right to a share of all food and to offerings of milk, cream, water and bread. It should hardly be surprising, therefore, to learn that they steal milk from herds of cows. They will also steal and kill animals from herds and flocks. In one case at Spanish Head, a *buggane* (or *cabbyl ushtey*) stole nearly an entire flock of sheep, reducing the farm to poverty. Eventually, the farmer's son bravely went in search of the thieving creature. He

---

202 *Manx Notes & Queries*, 1904, 122, 123 & 127.
203 Morrison, *Manx Fairy Tales*, 5.
204 Moore, *Folklore of the Isle of Man* 1891, c.3; Joseph Train, *Historical sketches*, vol.2 c.XVIII.
205 Campbell, *Popular Tales of the West Highlands*, vol.1, 81; Gill, *Second Manx Scrapbook*, c.6;

found its cave, which was full of the bones of the devoured sheep. He also found a sack, bearing his father's name, which contained gold and silver. In the circumstances, he felt entitled to take this, viewing it as a payment for the livestock consumed, and the farm's prosperity was thereby restored.[206]

In another story, a man realised that the someone was stealing potatoes from his field after dark. He decided to sit out all night to catch the culprit. He discovered it was the fairies and, by the next morning, he was white and shaking and only able to struggle home and get into his bed, where he soon died. This was the penalty for begrudging a few spuds to your faery neighbours.[207]

Livestock will sometimes be abducted to Faery by making it appear that they have died (just as is the case with humans, as we shall see later). One Manx witness described to Evans Wentz how her aunt saw a strange woman appear in the middle of a patch of gorse and then walk right over the top of the bushes to a heifer. She placed her hand on the cow and, within a few days, it had died.[208]

Even though the last case makes it clear that the *ferrishyn* make cattle (appear to) die in order to steal them, unlike Highland faeries the Manx little people don't seem to use elf-shot to kill beasts. These elf-shots are the flint arrow heads which are occasionally picked up on the island and they are evidently employed by the little people with some frequency, often to punish individuals who have offended them. Elf-shot were perceived as enough of a problem on the island for a charm (*pishag noi guint*) to have been formulated to avert injury by them:

---

[206] Leney, *Shadowland in Ellan Vannin,* 149; Gill, *Third Manx Scrapbook,* Part 2, c.3.
[207] Roeder, *Manx Folklore,* 1882.
[208] Evans-Wentz 122.

"Abraham lay at the feet of Jesus Christ.
'Arise up, Abraham,' said he, 'and walk along with me.'
'I cannot,' said he, 'for I am struck with elf-shot.'
If it came out of the air, let it turn back again;
and if it came out of the earth, let it return back again;
if it came under the tide of the sea, let it return again;
and if any evil-disposed person has wished, let it return upon himself again.
In the name of the Father, the Son, and Holy Ghost."[209]

There is an account which illustrates the use of shot against humans. A young man who unwisely followed a fairy pig was suddenly struck down with a sharp pain in his leg. This could only be relieved by a fairy healer, or charmer, who used a spell from a book to cast out the *guin* or stitch the youth was suffering (*guin shee* is elf-shot). It seems that the arrows may be used to abduct humans as well. In one account of a youth from Andreas, who was taken for four years by the fairies, he was able to protect his brothers from a similar fate. The two boys were out walking one day near a thorn bush when they heard a sharp crack which scared them so much that they immediately ran home. When their brother finally returned from his captivity, he told them that he had at that instant held up a plate to block a fairy arrow fired at them. Thorns (*drine*) were regarded as fairy haunts and it was said to be dangerous to sleep, or even to sit for too long, beneath one.[210]

---

209 Campbell, *Popular Tales of the West Highlands*, vol.1, 81; *Yn Lioar Manninagh*, vol. III, 157-91.
210 Morrison, *Manx Fairy Tales*, 100; Moore, *Folklore*, cc.3 & 7; Gill, *Manx Scrapbook*, c.4 'Ballaugh.'

Predicting the Future

The fairies seem to be able to see the future. I have mentioned already the adult sized fairies seen at Peel Castle whose shouting was a sign of bad weather approaching. If the fairy washer woman is seen, it foretells bad weather and we know of the ability of the merfolk to predict storms approaching. Many other fairy activities predict or warn of events to come.

In one strange account, a pregnant woman was in bed when seven or eight little women and a 'minister' entered the room. Because they could find no water, they baptised the child they had with them using some beer that happened to be brewing in the same room. The faery girl was named Joan, and the woman in her bed understood that this performance was a sign that she too would bear a girl. Mock christenings such as this were a common way of foretelling the sex of the unborn baby.[211]

The appearance of some faery beasts serves as a harbinger of death. For example, a clergyman out walking near his home heard a bull bellowing. He knelt and prayed and soon a beast larger than any normal bull passed him by, shaking the ground as it went. It disappeared towards a cottage and, when the priest went to the house, he found that the owner had died that very minute. In this case the *tarroo ushtey* he had seen had acted as a herald of death – or even its deliverer.[212]

It was also believed that a mock funeral procession, acted out by the faeries, would precede a death in the human community. In some cases, people have even been caught up in these proceedings and have had to help carry the bier. If the fairy carpenters are heard,

---
211 Waldron, *Isle of Man*, 39.
212 G. Waldron, *Isle of Man*, 34.

it will predict human deaths if they are engaged in making coffins rather than fishing gear. For instance, they were heard to be very busy shortly before a number of boats from Peel sank. Sometimes, the sound of approaching horse's hooves was sent by the fairies to warn of the imminent arrival of visitors.[213]

A regular ceremony that used to take place on New Year's Eve took advantage of the fairies' predictive powers. Before going to bed, a person would spread out the ashes from the hearth evenly and smoothly on the floor and the next morning, these would be inspected for traces of a faery footprint. If the mark of the foot had the toe pointing towards the door of the house, it was known that a family member would die that year. If the heel was towards the door, as if someone had entered the house, it was known that a new family member would be born that year.[214]

A strangely modern form of prognostication was reported from mid-Victorian times:

> "There was a man from Santon [whose] uncle of his used to see the fairies very often, while he was alive, and knew a great deal about them. He was often telling the people about the railway line, more than twenty years before anyone thought about it. He was seeing the fairies very often practising on it in the moonlight, and he could point out where the line was to be, as he was seeing fairy trains going along so often… The man said the railway line was made on the very spot he told them, more than twenty years before it was proposed."

This vision, like that of faery funerals, seems to demonstrate the fairy preference for conveying knowledge of the future to us by acting it out. Even so, it is a little odd that they should want to pass

---

213 Waldron, *Isle of Man*, 38; Gill, *Third Manx Scrapbook*, Part 2, c.3.
214 *Yn Lioar Manninagh*, vol.1, part 2, 290.

this information in this manner, seeing that they seem to have objected so vehemently to the outcome.[215]

Disrespecting Faeries

Given their strict moral code, and their attitude that humans are – in many respects – there to serve and satisfy the wishes of faeries, it will not seem out of character for them to react severely where they feel that their rights, privacy or dignity have been in some manner infringed. Sometimes the faery reactions may seem disproportionate to us. All we can do is to note – and respect – their displeasure.

Insults to fairies can elicit a very severe response: one night in 1830 a drunken man met some fairies dancing at Laxey. He swore at them and they chased him away by pelting him with gravel. This wasn't sufficient though: soon his horse and cow died and, within six weeks, he was dead himself. In comparison, a man called William Oates from Ballasalla got off very lightly. The fairies often entered his house and would play there on moonlit nights. One time they arrived just as he was going to bed, so he set out some fresh water for them – but he did so with the words "Now, little beggars, drink away." The water was thrown all over him for his impertinence.[216]

In the story of 'Billy Beg, Tom Beg and the Fairies,' hunchback cobbler Tom helped the fairy king and his troops and, as a reward, had his hump removed from his shoulders. Billy was a second hunchback cobbler who wanted to repeat the same feat and receive the same reward. However, in his overconfidence he insulted the fairies (by naming Sunday before them) and he ended up with Tom's hump added to his other shoulder.[217]

---

215 Gill, *Second Manx Scrapbook*, c.3.
216 *Isle of Man Times*, April 24th 1889, 4 'Antique Mona;' Cumming, *Isle of Man*, 1848, 30; Wentz 125.
217 Morrison, *Manx Fairy Tales*, 56.

Assaults upon the faeries or upon their property are always inadvisable. There used to be a little faery woman who was often seen around Maughold and who did spinning work for local families. One day a man released his dogs on her; the hounds surrounded the woman, scaring her terribly, but they would not touch her, so she was able to get to a nearby gully where she vanished. The man himself immediately fell ill and was unable to work for six months. Comparable is the case of a young man who, leaving the pub at Ballaglass one night, rather rashly tried to kick a little red woman whom he glimpsed darting out of sight under a gorse bush. A terrible pain immediately afflicted his leg and he was troubled by it and lame for the remainder of his life.[218]

In Malew parish near Orrisdale there is a tumulus called Fairy Hill. It is reported that a local farmer wanted to level the hillock but found it very difficult to persuade anyone to do the work for him. Eventually, two men agreed on the basis that they would be supplied with a keg of rum. Rather unwisely, this was delivered to the field before the work even began. One of the men took a drink to give himself courage for the job ahead, but then couldn't stop. He had to be carried home because he had got so drunk – and died on the way. His companion then became so scared that he abandoned the job – and the fairies' hill never did get flattened.[219]

As this last case demonstrates, the faeries expect that humans will show respect to ancient sites, with which they seem to have close links. Other cases confirm this. In 1888 it was reported that three coffins had recently been excavated at site in Castletown, a spot that had long been haunted but was no more after that date. Locals clearly saw that there was a direct linkage between the two events. In 1847 it was reported in the *Mona's Herald* that a man called Quayle,

---
218 Moore, *Folklore*, c.4; Gill, *Third Manx Scrapbook*, Part 2, c.3.
219 Gill, *Manx Scrapbook*, c.4 'Malew'.

living at Maughold, had had his house windows broken and the doors thrown open by the little people because he had ploughed up some land never before cultivated and, in so doing, had turned up bones from an old grave yard. The strong link between the fairies and ancient burial sites is further indicated by the experience of a man at Agneash, who saw between three and six of the little people at a spot where a man ploughing had lifted a number of burial cists. Mr Quayle's misfortunes were nothing compared to that of a man called Kewley, who levelled and ploughed up an old chapel covered with blackthorn, gorse and briar at The Rheyn, West Baldwin. Several of the family sickened and died, their prosperity vanished and the farm was plagued at night by noises, as if all the horses had been set loose in a panic.[220]

A person who disagrees with the fairies might expect to be ducked in a pool or dragged through hedges across the country side. Contempt and meanness are also disliked. A couple out walking once met a small, crippled man begging; he was dressed in rags and had crooked legs. Whilst the wife would have helped him, her husband refused to give any money, for which he was cursed by the fairy. They had a number of children subsequently – all the girls were born without disabilities, but all the boys were disabled just like the beggar. I mentioned a little earlier how a farmer was punished for trying to prevent the faeries taking a few of the potatoes from his fields. Miserliness is a trait the *ferrishyn* loathe.[221]

In an earlier section, we considered the duty of humans to share their food with the fairies and to leave bread and water out for them at night. Failure to do this will not be overlooked. I mentioned there

---

220 Waldron, *Isle of Man*, 38; *Yn Lioar Manninagh* vol.1, part 2, 290; A. Moore, *Folklore of the Isle of Man*, c.3; see Gill, *Manx Scrapbook*, c.4, 'Lezayre – Magher y Troddan' & 'Lonan – Agneash;' *Yn Lioar Manninagh*, vol. III, 482.
221 Gill, *Second Manx Scrapbook*, c.6; Roeder, *Manx Folklore*, 14; *Proceedings of the Isle of Man Natural History & Archaeology Society*, vol,1, Jan. 1889; *Yn Lioar Manninagh*, vol. II, 194; Gill, *Third Manx Scrapbook*, Part 2, c.3.

a servant girl living at Bride, who received a blow because she forgot the custom of making a little of the dough from a batch into an extra cake called the *soddhag rheynney*, the 'sharing or dividing cake,' which was baked by islanders specifically to give to the fairies, leaving for them it in the kitchen or just outside the main door. In a related story, a maid forgets to put out any water for the faeries, so in revenge they take a drop of blood from her toe to mix their bread dough. They eat most of the cakes they make but conceal bits of some under the cottage thatch before they leave at dawn. The next day the girl falls ill, but a visitor to the house who had overheard the faeries at their baking is able to cure her with some of the hidden cake crumbs.[222]

Food is a clearly a very sensitive subject to the *ferrishyn*. They spend a great deal of time taking it from humans, one way or another, and when humans consume faery food, they expect us to show proper appreciation. For instance, a man who stumbled upon a fairy feast, having followed the sound of music for miles across a large area of common land, was warned by one of the other diners (a man whom he thought he recognised and who was perhaps 'dead' in the human world) not to eat anything, or else he would never escape either. At the end of the feast, the man was given a silver cup full of wine; he poured the drink on the ground and, with a thunder clap, the banquet instantly vanished, leaving him alone with the cup. He donated the valuable goblet to his church.[223]

Refusing faery food in Faery is sensible, although it may attract their anger. Refusing it on earth is, in contrast, not advisable. Some faeries were one night in a house making *cowree* (an oatmeal dish). Each time the bowl emptied, they would spit in it and it would immediately refill. Two men present in the house were offered a

---

[222] Evans Wentz, *Fairy Faith*, 127-128; Roeder, *Manx Folktales*, 16.
[223] Waldron, *Description of the Isle of Man*, 27; *Manx Notes & Queries*, 1904, 30.

share. One accepted and ate happily; the other, perhaps put off by the repeated spitting, refused – and fell ill and died. In a variant of this story, two boys came home and saw through the window that the fairies were cooking the *cowree* in the kitchen. One declared that he'd eat what was left; his brother refused to do so – and sickened and died within the year.[224]

We have seen repeatedly that the words and symbols of the Christian faith are repulsive to faery kind, so anyone employing them deliberately is bound to upset them. A fiddler who was contracted to play at a fairy celebration over Christmas only realised what he'd agreed to when the man he'd been bargaining with sank into the ground once their deal had been concluded. The musician's parish priest advised him to keep his side of the bargain and attend, but to play only psalms. He did this – the party were outraged and the assembly vanished, leaving the fiddler on top of a high hill, so bruised and injured that it was a struggle for him to get home.[225]

In the previous cases, the humans involved have neglected an established obligation to the little people or have acted towards them rudely or violently. Sometimes, though, people infringe faery rules or property rights without intending or realising to do so. Sadly, their treatment as a result if frequently no less severe. A man who accidentally saw the fairies one night in a pea field near Jurby, witnessing a great crowd of little people dancing in red cloaks, was blinded for life by an old fairy woman who spotted him. A little boy who played on the fairy hill at Cronk Mooar was crippled for life: he never grew any taller and his mouth became twisted. Another young boy from Andreas went out bird-nesting. He passed a large briar bush and, as a result, his face "slipped all to one side." The local people said that this had been done by the fairies. Some English

---

224 *Yn Lioar Manninagh*, III; Roeder, *Manx Folktales*, 16.
225 Waldron, *Isle of Man*, 27.

folklore evidence suggests that there is some magical or faery power in briars – something that, by his proximity or some other perceived disrespect – the boy must have unwittingly violated.[226]

The *ferrishyn* are a shy and secretive people, so it is never sensible for humans to spy upon them. A man who watched fairies dancing in an old kiln was taken ill and was left unable to walk whilst another, who spied on them when they were dancing by looking through the keyhole of a deserted cottage, was blinded with a poke from the bow of the fiddle for his impertinence. We might say that the case of the farmer who stayed up to see who was stealing his potatoes was another example of spying upon the faeries punished; the *ferrishyn* may be happy to filch our goods, but they won't like to be watched whilst they're doing it.[227]

Whereas the faeries consider it wholly acceptable to take humans, both adults and children, kidnapping individual faeries will again meet with a stern response. A man caught a faery that hopped out of tree and took it home as a doll for his daughter, but as a result he became very ill. He was only able to cure himself by returning to the spot and setting the captive free.[228]

Finally, we should acknowledge that, whilst the fairies can make those they dislike ill, they equally have the power to cure the sick or to magically transmit their healing skills to humans, who will then be able to treat people or cattle – whether they have been made ill by the fairies themselves or by some more ordinary ailment.[229]

---

226 Wentz, 131; *Yn Lioar Manninagh* vol.III; *Choice Notes & Queries, Folklore*, 88 & 217; *Yn Lioar Manninagh*, vol.II, 194.
227 *Yn Lioar Manninagh*, III; Roeder, *Manx Folktales*, 7.
228 *Choice Notes & Queries*, 1859, 26.
229 Leney, *Shadowland*, 142; Moore, *Folklore*, c.3.

Changelings

Throughout the British Isles, the faeries have a dire reputation for stealing people of all ages. This is just as much as problem on Man as anywhere else and I will examine this by looking in turn at the taking of babies, children and adults.

Islanders used to say that the only human thing that the faeries coveted was babies and that it was always the prettiest who were abducted. For this reason, we can appreciate the incredible foolishness of the mother in this account: she had a little baby who was crying uncontrollably and couldn't be comforted in the middle of the night. Exasperated, she lifted him up and said: "Here fairies, take him." This was meant to frighten the child into calming down, but that moment the bed was struck by a great blow, which shook the mother and father and frightened them both very much.[230]

Because of the very real risk of faery abduction, babies were protected by marking them with soot. It seems highly probable that this would have involved a cross on the forehead, which, if correct, would have invoked the power of the Christian religion combined with the efficacy of burnt material against the fairies (burning turves have often been used as protection, for example). If parents had to go out and leave their children behind, they would be safeguarded by placing on their cradles a bible, the (iron) fire tongs, a rowan cross (made without using an iron blade and ideally from a branch with its red berries still attached) or their father's trousers "why exactly the latter are effective is very hard to explain). Another protective measure was tying a red thread around the baby's neck. Of course, early baptism is the surest protection but, even when going to the

---

[230] *Yn Lioar Manninagh*, vol.4, 161; Moore, *Folklore of the Isle of Man*, 1891, c.3; *Manx Notes & Queries*, 1904, 121.

church, the mother would carry bread and cheese with her as an additional defence, giving it to the first person she met.[231]

It appeared that various tricks were used by the little people to distract watchful humans and to create an opportunity to snatch a baby. A cry of 'fire' might be heard, disturbing a household and giving the fairies a chance to slip in and seize the child whilst the parents' attention was distracted. In one family's case this happened twice and each time, after it was realised that there had been a false alarm, the baby had been found dropped on the threshold – the fairies had been disturbed before the theft was complete. Only on a third occasion did their plan succeed.[232]

Because new-born babies (and their mothers, who were often desired by the fairies as wet nurses) were so vulnerable to being taken, a range of community measures were developed to protect mother and child. The Manx practice was to provide 'blithe meat' (oatbread and cheese) for people who came to visit a mother and her new-born baby. A portion of this would be scattered around for the unseen visitors, too – partly perhaps to win their favour as 'godmothers' and partly to guard against the risk of abduction. One man recalled in Edwardian times how, when he was a boy, his mother had been in bed after childbirth when a fairy woman entered the house, obviously intent on snatching the new born. The boy had gone into the bedroom to take a bit of the bread and cheese and luckily interrupted the woman just as she trying to drag his mother out of her bed.[233]

In one Manx case a woman was in bed nursing her week-old baby when two old women she didn't know entered the room. They

---

231 Gill, *Second Manx Scrapbook*, c.3; *Proceedings of the Isle of Man Natural History & Archaeological Society*, vol.1, Jan.1889; Waldron, *Isle of Man*, fn.49; Moore, *Folklore*, c.3; Herbert, *Isle of Man*, 194; Wentz 124; *Yn Lioar Manninagh* vol.1, part 2, 289.
232 Waldron, *Isle of Man*, 30–39.
233 *Manx Notes & Queries*, 1904, 197; *Yn Lioar Manninagh*, vol.3; Herbert. *Isle of Man*, 194.

tried to seize the infant from her, in response to which the woman blessed herself. Her assailants vanished instantly, but they left finger marks on the child's heel which were visible until she died in old age. In a similar case, the woman was alone in bed with her baby when she felt the newborn being pulled out of her arms and heard the sound of the fairies rushing away. She cried out god's name, which repelled them before the child was taken, but she saw the table beside the bed spin around twenty times before the noise of the faeries subsided.[234]

In another very typical case, a confined mother was being watched over at night by two local women. They kept feeling drowsy and, as they started to fall asleep, the candle in the room would dim. The pair would then awaken with a start, brought on by their fear of the fairies, and the flame would flare up again. This happened several times until they awoke to find the expectant mother out of bed and an argument taking place outside. The fairies had been in the act of taking the pregnant woman but the neighbour's waking had disturbed and defeated them. In a further case, a woman was in bed with her husband after her confinement. She heard a voice outside call her name and answered it automatically. Instantly, a man was in the room standing over her and declaring "Thy flesh is mine, thy blood is mine." She had the presence of mind to bless herself and he vanished.[235]

It was usual faery practice to replace the human baby with a faery, whether that was a baby or perhaps an elderly person needing considerable care. These substitutes were called 'changelings' (*lhiannoo caghlaait* in Manx). Because a member of the faery community was being left in a human household, they wanted to be sure that it would be well looked after, as is demonstrated by

---

[234] *Yn Lioar Manninagh*, vol.4, 161; Wentz 120.
[235] Roeder, *Manx Folktales*, 1 & 11.

one interesting incident. A woman went to harvest corn in a field and laid her baby down whilst she worked. Seeing an opportunity, a little red faery woman snatched the child up and set a changeling in its place. The elf-child cried out and the human mother naturally started to go to pick up what she thought was still her infant. One of the men in the field prevented her and, when it became apparent that the exchange had been discovered and that the changeling was going to be being ignored, the faery woman replaced the human baby and departed.[236]

In a very similar case, a woman went to help with the reaping, taking her un-christened child with her. She placed it between two sheaves on the headland of the field (the unploughed strip at the end of the rows), taking the precaution of placing an open pair of scissors across it (iron in the shape of a cross), for fear the fairies should take it. She was busy at the other end of the furrows when she heard the baby wailing, and thinking that something had happened to the child, she hastened to the spot where she had placed it, but found that it wasn't there. Half distracted with fear, she ran towards field gate, from where she saw two little people dragging the child along between them. She at once rushed after them, seized her baby back and carried it safely home. It was supposed that the scissors had slipped off, and thus left the child unprotected.[237]

Sometimes, instead of a live substitute, the faeries left a facsimile made of wood in the cradle, called a stock. In an account recorded by Evans Wentz, a man was out riding at night when he came across a little baby lying in the road. He took it home for his wife to care for but, by the time he got there, he found he was carrying only a block of wood. This was evidently a 'stock' that had been made by the fairies with a view to stealing a human child. The fairies were

---
236 *Choice Notes & Queries*, 1859, 26; Gill, *Third Manx Scrapbook*, Part 2, c.3..
237 Moore, *Folklore*, c.3.

then heard outside, yelling angrily at the man, presumably annoyed because their planned abduction had been disrupted.[238]

It was understood across the British Isles and Ireland that changeling babies were easily identified by their suddenly wizened appearance and poor temperaments or by their preternatural knowledge and abilities (as they were really very old). What's more, they usually had voracious appetites, yet never grew or developed. George Waldron described a couple of Manx changelings that he saw during the 1720s. These are his accounts:

> "I was prevailed upon myself to go and see a child, who, they told me, was one of these changelings, and indeed I must own I was not a little surprised, as well as shocked, at the sight. Nothing under heaven could have a more beautiful face; but though between five and six years old, and seemingly healthy, he was so far from being able to walk, or stand, that he could not so much as move any one joint: his limbs were vastly long for his age, but smaller than an infant's of six months; his complexion was perfectly delicate, and he had the finest hair in the world; he never spoke, nor cried, eat scarce anything, and was very seldom seen to smile, but if any one called him a fairy elf, he would frown and fix his eyes so earnestly on those who said it, as if he would look them through. His mother, or at least his supposed mother, being very poor, frequently went out a charring, and left him a whole day together. The neighbours, out of curiosity, have often looked in at the window to see how he behaved when alone, which, whenever they did, they were sure to find him laughing, and in the utmost delight. This made them judge that he was not without company more pleasing to him than

---

238 Wentz 127.

any mortal's could be; and what made this conjecture seem the more reasonable was, that if he were left ever so dirty, the woman at her return, saw him with a clean face, and his hair combed with the utmost exactness and nicety."

It's interesting to note in this case that, although the fairy child has been left with humans, it is still cared for by its relatives. In another Manx case, the fairies managed to swap the baby, after which the mother:

> "saw something like a child, but far different from her own, who was a very beautiful, fat, well-featured babe; whereas, what was now in the room of it, was a poor, lean, withered deformed creature. It lay quite naked, but the clothes belonging to the child that was exchanged for it, lay wrap't up all together on the bed. This creature lived with them near the space of nine years, in all which time it ate nothing except a few herbs, nor was ever seen to void any other excrement than water; it neither spoke, nor could stand or go, but seemed enervate in every joint, like the changeling I mentioned before, and in all its actions showed itself to be of the same nature."[239]

Contrasted to these accounts, in which the changelings seem to have been suffering from physical or mental disabilities, there is a Manx story of a woman from Rushen whose beloved child was a hunchback. The little people replaced it with a beautiful and happy faery baby. The woman grieved so much for the loss of her own child that the changeling was swapped back again. This is obviously good news, but the fairies had always visited her home previously because she put out water at night and offered a little dough when she was baking. They never returned again, perhaps taking their

---

239 Waldron, *Isle of Man*, 30–39.

luck with them. Generally, however, the original child was never returned and the unfortunate parent just had to bring up the changeling as his/her own. One woman cared for such a fairy child for eighteen years, during which time it never spoke or walked.[240]

If it was suspected that a changeling had been substituted for a human child, there were various ways of exposing the faery. In one case, the suspected changeling was laid across a pot containing urine, which was being allowed to go stale for use in laundering clothes. The creature, which looked like an old man, wailed at this and the strategy quickly worked, because after a short wait the sound of the crying changed and the mother found her own child restored to her.[241]

In a very similar account, the changeling nature of the child was exposed to his family by a visiting tailor, for whom the boy offered to dance, and they promptly took the necessary steps to banish the fairy infant, building up the fire in order to scare the supernatural away. The 'baby' leapt out of his cradle when he saw what was being prepared and ran out of the house. The mother then saw "a flock of low-lying clouds shaped like gulls chasing each other away up Glen Rushen," along with whistles and wicked laughter. Her true son then returned to her. Another version of these events ends less happily, with the baby dancing away with the tailor. In this telling, it would appear that the tailor could have been a fairy himself and that they both returned to the fairy hill together. In either version, though, the unnatural knowledge and ability of the child demonstrates that it is really an aged fairy in an infant's body.[242]

---

240 *Royal Cornwall Gazette,* 17/8/1899, 6; A. Herbert, *The Isle of Man,* 1909, 174; *Choice Notes & Queries – Folklore,* 1859, 26.
241 *Yn Lioar Manninagh,* vol.3.
242 Morrison, 'A Manx Changeling Story,' *Folklore,* vol.21, 1910, 472 & *Manx Fairy Tales,* 85; *Manx Notes & Queries,* 1904, no.132; *Yn Lioar Manninagh,* vol.1, 323–8.

As this last case shows us, once the changeling had been uncovered, very firm measures were used to scare the faeries into bringing the human baby back. Extreme violence, whether beating, burning or attempted drowning, were all used to drive out the impostor baby. A case reported from Foxdale combined both fire and water, to be absolutely sure of expelling the changeling, it seems. The mother had heard a great bustle outside, as if a great crowd of people were walking around her house, so she opened the door and looked out, but saw nothing. When she came in again her baby was screaming in the cradle, so she went to feed it, but was surprised to see that her own fair child had changed into a dark little thing of skin and bones. The family cared for the baby as best they could, but he was always unsettled and crying and was unable to sit up on his own, unsupported. A neighbour tried to persuade the parents that this was really a substituted fairy, and wanted to try some tests on him, but the mother for a long time resisted this. At length she agreed, so they went to a river bank and laid a lot of dry gorse in a circle. They put the child on some dry straw in the middle of the circle and set fire to the gorse. He lay quietly until the straw began to burn, but then he started to tumble around, rolling out of the ring in a place where the fire had not yet caught. The child then went on turning over and over down the hill toward the river. Just before he rolled into the water the mother ran and picked him up. She saved the baby from drowning, but she had to care for him for many years afterwards, until he faded away to a skeleton and finally died. The changeling was buried but her own baby was never returned.[243]

Great cruelty could be involved in these cases. The measures used are obviously illegal now, but even in the past some people objected to the methods. At Niarbyl, in Patrick parish, there lived a family whose child was understood to be a changeling. He had the wizened visage characteristic of his kind, kept shaking his head

---
[243] *Manx Notes & Queries,* 1904, no.131.

from side to side all day long, and, when anybody took notice of him, he would look up the chimney. Though he was old enough to speak, no-one ever heard him say a word. A visitor to the house advised his parents to burn him, telling them that when the fairies heard his screams, they would take him away and bring back the child they had stolen. The family had built up the materials for the fire out of doors in front of the house, and were just taking hold of the child, in spite of his struggles, when some of the neighbours intervened and put a stop to it.[244]

The very young are preferred, but children of all ages are at risk of being taken.

Faery Abductions of Children

Across Britain, the faeries have an unfortunate propensity for kidnapping children. There is plenty of evidence for the prevalence of this practice on the Isle of Man.

May Eve is an especially risky time, when children are most vulnerable to being taken. Nonetheless, it is dangerous at any season of year for children to eat or drink with the fairies and, if they do, they are likely to be kept by them for seven years (though the interval may feel much shorter for the abductee: as the fairies say in one of Dora Broome's children's stories, "It is always today with us"). Another apparent way of entrapping children is to cut their hair, which is regarded by the fairies as gold. Children who long too much to see the fairies are also at great risk of having their wishes granted.[245]

Many children are snatched without ceremony, whenever an opportunity to abduct them arises. In one case, a boy sent at night to

---
244 Gill, *Manx Scrapbook,* c.4 'Patrick.'
245 Leney, *Shadowland in Ellan Vannin;* Broome, *More Fairy Tales,* 8, 14, 30, 35 & 42.

a neighbour's house to borrow some candles was chased on his way home by a small woman and boy. He ran, but only just kept ahead of them, and even when he had reached the safety of his home, he had lost the power of speech, his hands and feet were twisted awry and his finger nails had grown very long in just a minute. He remained this way for a week until a 'fairy doctor' was called, a person who could work charms and who grew medicinal herbs (often in a 'fairy garden'). Whilst awaiting the doctor's arrival, a neighbour decided to burn the boy with a piece of glowing turf held in a pair of tongs, to see if he could be exposed as a changeling or the faeries might be provoked into reacting. The strategy seemed to work, for the fairies swapped the boy back again in response to the burn. The recovered child was only able to say that he had been conscious of being carried off by the fairies, but knew no more after that.[246]

Another adventitious attempt at kidnapping was described by woman from Ballasalla to George Waldron in about 1730. She told him how her ten-year-old daughter had met a large crowd of little people up on the mountains. Some of the group had tried to abduct her but others had objected to this and had tried to protect the girl. As a result of this, some of the faeries had fallen to fighting. Some of the other fairies then spanked her for being the cause dissension amongst them. When she got home, she had distinct prints of tiny hands on her buttocks.[247]

Some children seem to be singled out for abduction and the faeries diligently work towards their goal over a period of time. A girl at Lezayre became thin and listless. Her mother suspected that she had got involved with the little people and had been 'fairy struck,' so she watched the girl one night. The woman discovered that her daughter was going out nightly and dancing with the fairies

---
246 Evans Wentz 132.
247 Waldron, *Isle of Man*, 39.

on a nearby hill. In due course, the child died, but she was believed really to have gone to live with the little people permanently. This story reflects in tragic terms the malign influence that contact with the fairies can have on a child. Writer Dora Broome expressed this in memorable terms: a mother warns her daughter that the fairies would never cease to try to claim her permanently: "Drawing and drawing thee, they'd be… and no peace at thee, night or day, but thou must be up and away with them…"[248]

A fascinating report describes how the fairies steadily tried to steal a girl's soul from her body – and how her mother counteracted their efforts. The account is relayed in verse form:

> *The Fairies*
> "Drawing, whilst the dame did snore,
> Her daughter's vitals from the core
> Into an heirloom china mug,
> Then laid it 'neath the chimney lug
> That while it withered day by day,
> The virgin, too, would pine away."

> *The Cure*
> This night at twelve, come here alone,
> And underneath this very stone
> You'll find a china mug or cup,
> Which you will take, then break it up
> And throw the pieces in the fire,
> Then quickly to your bed retire."

The scenario described here is clear enough, but it is a little hard to explain in traditional faery-lore terms. It would seem to be a combination of the idea that the fairies can extract the essential

---

248 Gill, *Second Manx Scrapbook,* c.6; Broome, *More Fairy Tales,* 15.

goodness from items such as foodstuffs, along with the idea of a 'separable soul' that can be hidden away from the body. Clearly, if the mother can locate where her daughter's spirit is concealed, she can free her from the enchantment.[249]

Faery Abductions of Adults

Babies and children are generally most desirable, but adults are sometimes taken, perhaps because they have a skill the faeries desire (such as being talented musicians), because they are required to undertake manual labour for the fairies or, perhaps, simply because it amuses the little people to do it.

Kidnappings seem to happen in several ways. For example, in one case a woman was surrounded on the road by the faeries and jostled in a direction she didn't want to go; she only managed to free herself from this by calling her son.[250]

A man from Glen Maye used to go fishing with a partner at Peel. Their habit was for one to pick up the other each morning by whistling outside his house as he passed. One day the second man heard the whistle and set out as usual, but he was never seen again, although his voice was sometimes heard crying for help in the glen. The fairies had taken him by imitating his friend's whistle. Presumably part of the trick was that the man voluntarily went with them.[251]

The risk of voluntarily putting yourself in the faeries' power is seen in the next case as well. Two men joined a fairy dance in a house. After a while one went outside to relieve himself against the wall of the cottage and it instantly disappeared – along with his companion inside. The latter was only rescued from the dance

---

249 *Yn Lioar Manninagh* vol.III, 156.
250 Evans Wentz, *Fairy Faith*,126.
251 Gill, *Third Manx Scrapbook*, Part 2, c.3.

seven years later, at which point he complained about having to go home so soon. In another version of this story, one of the pair drinks some wine before joining the dance. He is then unable to leave for another year. In a further related incident, the man relieving himself couldn't find his way back into the house and when dawn came, he found that he was alone and stranded on top of a mountain. In two of these cases, we are reminded that time passes differently in Faery to the human world.[252]

As with children, some kidnappings of adults appear to be premeditated. A young man, who lived in Fistard, used to go with the fairies every night, coming home exhausted in the morning. His family couldn't keep him in the house and he would sometimes tell them of the fun he had with the fairies, how they would turn him to a horse and ride on his back, describing the nice whips the fairies had and how sharply they cracked them. The youth carried on that way for several years, but died before he was twenty. The front teeth in his mouth grew overlarge and he became very strange to look at – like a horse, perhaps.[253]

As this last case reveals, some people are known to be taken and ridden all night across the countryside, equipped with blinkers just like a real horse. This faery habit is known from one Scottish story, but it is a particular vice of the Manx little people. The faeries' victims feel no weight on their backs during their experience, but they become tired for loss of sleep and thin and weak from their exertions. Wearing a flower or herb should be enough to prevent this. For example, a woman realised that her son was getting very thin. She stayed up at night to watch him and found that the fairies were taking him to ride until dawn. She treated him with one of the protective herbs listed earlier and he was not abducted again.

---

252 *Yn Lioar Manninagh*, III.
253 *Manx Notes & Queries*, 124

One of Evans Wentz' witnesses described how a relative's friend was regularly taken, being snatched as he walked home from work in the evening and ridden all night over fields and hedges, leaving him exhausted and unable to work then next morning.[254]

A woman at Glenchass had been confined and was in bed, and a light was burning in the room; her husband was lying beside her, fast asleep. She heard a troop of feet coming up the stairs and the sound of a log being dragged. Soon, she saw a large number fairies peeping in at the door; then they entered and started to make a human image from the log. She kept trying to wake her husband up, but he was very hard to rouse. Luckily, before the form they were making was quite finished, she was able to wake him and, as soon as they heard his voice, the faeries left as fast as possible, dragging the image after them: the couple heard it bumping on the steps as they ran down. It seems that what was happening here was that the faeries were making a stock, the figure that is substituted for the stolen person and which gives the impression that they are either dead or perhaps ill and unconscious or in a coma. In this case, it looks as though the woman was wanted, perhaps as a wet nurse or perhaps so that her baby would have been born in Faery.[255]

A similar incident occurred at Ballalece, where a farmer's wife was abducted by the fairies, who left a dead carcase in her place. The woman returned briefly after a period of time and was able to tell her husband that she would ride past in a cavalcade of horses one night and he would be able to seize her bridle and rescue her permanently. However, this would only work provided that the barn floor had been swept completely clean. The husband did as he was instructed, but the rescue failed. The reason for this is that, after his wife disappeared, he had remarried and his second wife overheard

---

254 C. Roeder, *Manx Folk Tales*, 11–12; *Yn Lioar Manninagh*, vol.1, part 2, 290; Wentz 121.
255 *Manx Notes & Queries*, 126; Gill, *Third Manx Scrapbook*, Part 2, c.3.

the first wife's instructions and had sabotaged the plan – by hiding a straw under a bushel on the barn floor, so that first wife's magical condition was not satisfied.[256]

Some adults are taken by the fairies only temporarily, perhaps for their amusement or perhaps as a punishment for some offence that the person has committed, knowingly or not. Often, these takings involve carrying people through the air at great height – strongly suggesting that it is meant as some sort of sanction. One Manx writer described those taken as being carried 'insensible' through the sky, a statement that also tells us that the Manx fairies can get around by flying if they wish to. As an example, a man from Fleshwick was walking one night when he encountered a *buggane*. He climbed over a hedge to avoid it, but instead found himself caught up by the fairies and forced to run as fast as he could over the fields until he got to a cliff edge, where the fays suddenly deposited him.[257]

The Ballalece case just discussed shows us that it is possible for people to be rescued from faery captivity. A fascinating example of this took place at Magher y Breck in Maughold parish. A young man brought his new bride home after their wedding but, the very same night, she was stolen by the fairies of Clagh Hoit. As soon as she was missed, everybody guessed what had happened to her and the bridegroom went straight away to the nearby fairy hill and demanded her back from a fairy-man, who was walking about outside it. The fairy refused to give her up and retired into his stronghold, shutting the door in the new husband's face. The young groom vowed that he would get her out next morning, even if he had to dig down to the roots of Clagh Hoit itself. He gathered all the men he could find, armed them with picks and spades, and set them to work. After they had been digging for a while the same fairy man appeared and

---

256 Jenkinson, *Practical Guide*, 60; 'The Lost Wife' in F. Angwin, *Manx Folk Tales*, 2015.
257 Waldron, *Isle of Man*, 27; Roeder, *Manx Folktales*, 9.

promised to yield the bride up if the husband and his party would go away, so as not to see where and how she came out. She returned home the same day, but did not know she had been away at all.[258]

Being with the Faeries

The relatives of abducted people are obviously distraught at their loss and desperate to recover their loved ones. What is the experience of being taken like for the victims, though?

The evidence we have suggests that contact with the faeries need not be wholly unpleasant. For instance, some men walking along a road one night met three huge fairies coming the other way. As they passed them, the men felt a curious sensation, as if 'lifted up' and they felt "terrible curious." A very similar sounding experience was recounted by a Mr J. H. Kelly to Evans Wentz in 1910. The witness had been walking back from Laxey to Douglas one moonlit night when he heard voices and "was conscious of being in the midst of an invisible throng." The strange feeling continued for the distance of a mile or so: he had the sensation that invisible beings were with him yet "there was no fear or emotion or excitement, but perfect calm on my part," he recalled. Eventually he turned off the main road and "there was a sudden and strange quietness and a sense of isolation came over me, as though the joy and peace of my life had departed with the invisible throng." This experience left him convinced of the reality of the fairy folk.[259]

A Manx youth was taken by the faeries for a space of four years. He said that, whilst he was away, he could still see his friends and family, but he could not be seen by them nor could he communicate with them in any way. When he returned to this world, he said it was like awaking from unconsciousness. This latter remark suggests

---
258 Gill, *Manx Scrapbook,* c.4, 'Maughold.'
259 *Yn Lioar Manninagh* III; Wentz 134.

some of the confusion and disorientation that contact with the faeries can cause.[260]

Faery Mischief

As described when discussing abductions of humans, some takings seem to be carried out just for the fairies' amusement. Without doubt, there is a strong vein of mischief in their characters.

An example of what seems to be pure mischief, intended solely to vex and exasperate the human, is found in the story of a midwife who had assisted at the birth of a fairy child. After the successful delivery, she was offered food by the new father. On a table he placed two oatcakes, one whole and one broken, inviting her to eat whichever she liked as long as it was neither the whole nor the broken cake. When she plaintively queried what in God's name she was supposed to eat, the scene vanished and she found herself alone on a mountain side.[261]

It appears that faery dancing might also be used as an opportunity for mischief as well as for pleasure. One night in 1884 a postman found his horse and cart surrounded by a group of faeries dressed in what he described as red suits and holding lanterns. They encircled him, dancing around in a ring, and proceeded to throw the mail sacks out of the cart into the road. As fast as the postman replaced them, the little people threw them out again. This went on for nearly four hours until sunrise.[262]

In a Manx version of the common British nuisance boggart story, the troublesome *ferrishyn* used to eat all the food in Ballacaine farm's kitchen, or else they would make noise all night, keeping the farm

---
260 Moore, *Folklore*, c.3; Rhys, *Manx Folklore*, Part One.
261 Wentz 127.
262 Bord, *Fairies*, 42–43; W. Martin, 'Collectanea – Goblins in the Isle of Man,' *Folklore*, vol.13, 1902, 186.

servants awake. These little people wore the typical red clothes and green hats of the Manx fairies and the servants were, apparently, scared that they might be turned into fairies themselves if they spent too long in their company. Eventually, it was resolved to catch all the troublesome fairies, bundle them into a barrel and chuck them in the sea. Ballacaine was fairy free after that. The violent conclusion to this story reminds us that faeries are not necessarily immortal and indestructible after all.[263]

Finally, we have a few examples of what would, in Cornwall or Devon, be unhesitatingly labelled pixy-leading. A young woman was going home from Howe Chapel one evening. Her route was across a field or two, but the night was fine and not dark, so she was not afraid to cross the fields alone. She started without problems until she went over the stile into the field and along the path towards the next stile, but when she came to the hedge where that stile should have been, she couldn't find it, and the hedge was so high that she couldn't climb over it either. She started going round the hedge looking for the stiles, but she could find neither of them, nor any spot in the boundary that she could climb. At last, she was very weary, and wanted to sit down and rest herself, but there seemed to be something urging her to walk, so she kept walking around and around the field for the whole of the long wintry night until she was so tired that she could hardly drag her feet. When dawn came at last, she found herself in the little field next her own house, and the stile in the same spot as it always was, and the hedge low enough to get over anywhere.[264]

Returning from Port Erin one winter's night, some travellers were proceeding very well until they got to the notorious Crosh Molley Mooar. There, suddenly, they couldn't tell where they were

---

263 Roeder, *Manx Folk Tales*, 23.
264 *Manx Notes & Queries*, 1904, 187.

and couldn't see anything. The party found themselves climbing precipices on hands and knees and stumbling into deep pools of water – features they should not have encountered on their route. Fortunately, after a little while they saw a bright light, made towards it, and found it to be their destination. Another traveller, coming home from Port Erin one moonlit night in the mid-1870s had a very similar experience in exactly the same place. He reached a point where he could see the road very plainly going towards Crosh Molley Mooar, but when he proceeded along it, he was unable to reach Crosh Molley, even after walking for a considerable time. He realised he had no idea where he was heading and then, suddenly, found himself back at start again. He headed towards Crosh Molley a second time and then got past it without any difficulty at all.[265]

These incidents of having fun with hapless humans, by changing the landscape, hiding gates and stiles and leading them in endless circles are very typical of the sorts of nuisance which faeries so enjoy throughout the British Isles. What's notable, however, is that in none of these Manx examples is there mention of the victims turning their coats or other garments to dispel the fairy influence. It looks as though this widespread remedy was not known on the Isle of Man: instead, carrying either salt or a *bollan* bone with you was the recommended protection – but, of course, you had to remember to prepare in advance. Perhaps the travellers in the cases described forgot the necessary precautions before they set out. Even so, there isn't always time to get ready: a man living at Fleshwick went outside one night to pass water before he went to sleep; he was unable to find his house again and, when dawn came, he was on top of Bradda mountain, a mile away, although he had no sense of having travelled any distance.[266]

---

265 *Manx Notes & Queries*, 1904, 189.
266 *Yn Lioar Manninagh*, vol.III.

Faery Music

The Manx fairies are passionately fond of music, "particularly that of light and festive character which best accords with their reputed habits," according to Waldron. Its sound has the power to spell bind listeners for extended periods, often detaining them so long that, when they get back home, they find that that several days have passed like minutes and there has been a total change during their absence. The *ferrishyn* are great musicians themselves, but they will kidnap human fiddle players whenever the opportunity arises, often by luring them into one of their hills with the sound of their music.[267]

A man called Willy the Fairy (William Cain) was known on Man in late Victorian and Edwardian times; he lived at Rhenass Farm near Cronk yr Voddy and often heard fairies singing and playing instruments in Glen Helen at night. He had even learned some songs from listening to these fairies. In fact, quite a number of tunes and songs are reported to have been borrowed by humans, being fairy compositions originally. They are remarkably hard to record though: another musician reportedly had to return three times to the same spot where he'd heard faery music to be able to commit a melody to memory. It's only very occasionally that humans are able to learn a faery tune and then contribute it to the mortal repertoire.[268]

Fairy music has been heard at a variety of locations across the island. Waldron stated that music could be heard around the huge standing stone at Devil's Den, Barrule. George Gelling, a joiner of Ballasalla, in 1910 described how he had twice heard fairy music coming from the vicinity of Rushen Abbey. "They were playing tunes not of this world," he recalled, "and on each occasion I

---

267 Waldron, *Isle of Man*, fn.53; *Manx Notes & Queries*, 1904, 116; Broome, *Fairy Tales*, 65; 'The Fiddler & The Fairy Folk,' in F. Angwin, *Manx Folk Tales*.
268 Gill, *Second Manx Scrapbook*, cc. 6 & 8; Evans Wentz, *The Fairy Faith* 118 & 131 – two examples from Man; Moore, *Folklore*, c.3; Rhys, *Manx Folklore*, Part One.

listened for nearly an hour." As this comment tells us, the nature of faery music is that it is ethereal and bewitching. George Waldron reported that in the 1720s islanders would hear "Musick, as could proceed from no earthly instruments." Its effect can be to freeze people and animals to the spot whilst it lasts, for periods of up to forty-five minutes. Waldron described how an English gentleman he knew had once been riding over Douglas bridge when he heard "the finest Symphony, I will not say in the World, for nothing human ever came up to it. The Horse was no less sensible of the Harmony than himself, and kept an immoveable Posture all the Time it lasted..." This man, a former sceptic, was converted by this experience to a true believer in the existence of the Manx fairies. We may also note – once again – how horses are at least as sensitive as humans to the faery presence.[269]

As mentioned earlier, the habit of the little people is often to dance and play music in people's homes at night. However gorgeous the tunes may be, therefore, they can also be a great nuisance and disturbance. An old man at Ballacaine was kept awake night after night by the sound of fairy music in his house. Finally, he'd had enough; he could hear them tuning their fiddles so he got up and went down and asked if he could join the dancing too. He enjoyed a few reels with his visitors and then was able to fall fast asleep. He was never troubled by the fairies making merry in his house again and it was said that this was because he had shown good humour. If he had stormed in, shouting and complaining at the intrusions and constant disturbance, he would probably have suffered until his dying day.[270]

---

269 Waldron, *Isle of Man*, 65, 37 & footnote 53; Evans Wentz 124 & 69.
270 Roeder, *Manx Folktales*, 24.

Faery Gold

The faeries are often reported to dispense gold and silver to favoured individuals or, conversely, to hoard their wealth away from greedy human eyes. It's never entirely clear where these riches come from – or even whether they're actually real.

Much of our evidence suggests that the Manx fairies have no need for hard cash at all: they steal a great deal from their human neighbours, as we've seen, and they are also known to work for payments in kind. The *fynoderee* is content with bread and milk, for example, whilst other fairies will assist with the dairy work on farms in return for a little of the butter or cheese.[271]

All the same, there is some evidence that the *ferrishyn* also engage in normal commercial activities with humans. For example, a farmer taking a horse to market was met by a small man who asked to buy the steed. A bargain was struck between the pair, after which the buyer mounted his new horse – and promptly sank into the earth. The seller sought the advice of a priest upon the cash he'd received, but was told it was safe to keep it as it had come from a fair deal. Somewhat similar is a story concerning a little girl who comes across a fairy market: the stall-holders accept locks of her blonde hair in payment for sweets as they say that it is 'fairy gold.' Nevertheless, the same account warns that, full though the fair was of delightful and tempting gifts and foods, it was really all an illusion created for the purpose of catching a human being.[272]

We can be certain, even so, that the fairies understand all about doing deals with people. A woman was at home preparing a meal when a little old woman in red whom she did not know appeared at the door and asked for a loan of meal and promised to return

---
271 Leney, *Shadowland*, 147.
272 Waldron, *Isle of Man*, 34; Broome, *More Fairy Tales*, 8–15.

every grain. The woman came back the next day with some flour and advised the housewife to wrap it in cloth and set it aside in a hole, after which she would never want for grain or flour. After a while, the red woman returned and asked that the farmer change around the way his cows were stabled in the byre, putting their troughs where their tails had been and so preventing their waste running down into the fairies' home beneath. At first, the farmer refused, but then all his cows fell sick, so he complied and all went well again.[273]

It is also beyond question that the fairies are aware of humans' greatest weakness, our greed for gold, and are fully prepared to exploit it. They know that, for gold, we might do almost anything and that we may be prepared to act recklessly to gain it, not thinking of our safety. For instance, a Manx girl walking over a bridge on the island was offered a farthing by three little men. Wisely she refused, knowing that she'd have been carried off if she had accepted it. Temptation – and even an element of selling her soul – were evidently involved here.[274]

The Manx fairies are reported to lead some people to buried treasure, but they are just as likely to taunt our avarice to possess wealth. In one case, the fairies whispered to a man drowsing on his sofa about hidden gold; in shock he fell onto the floor, was ill for the next six months and was lamed for the remainder of his life.[275]

It's also fair to add that the faeries can be just as avaricious and protective of their riches as any human. A man once stole a silver cup from a feast at Cronk Mooar. The fairies were, predictably, outraged and pursued him. He escaped by wading along the river there; the fairies called on him to walk on the stones, but he stayed in the water, and got away, clearly indicating that crossing flowing water is

---

273 Roeder, *Manx Folktales*, 15.
274 *Choice Notes & Queries – Folklore*, 1859, 26.
275 *Choice Notes & Queries – Folklore*, 26; Morrison, *Manx Fairy Tales*, 1–2.

a problem for the *ferrishyn*. A variant of this story involves the man being pursued as far as a cow shed; there he was able to sprinkle the cows' urine (*mooin ollee*) at the doorway and around the walls as a defence against the fairies until dawn. In a second story on the same theme, a young man stole a hoard of fairy gold so that he could get married, but in revenge the fairies abducted him for seven years on his wedding night. His wife remarried in his absence, thinking that he had died or deserted her, so that even when he returned, he could not resume the life he had left behind.[276]

The Lhiannan Shee

On the Isle of Man, the faery lover, the *lhiannan shee*, is a very strong tradition, albeit it much more prevalent in the south of the island. *Lhiannan shee* are especially dangerous, but love for any supernatural is a perilous affair. We have already seen the problems of loving mermaids; another, rather less predictable problem was mentioned by Dora Broome in one of her stories: a man spoke the words of a charm and was taken into the fairy hill at Port Erin, where he fell in love with his own grandmother, who had gone to live there with them, as is said to be the fate of many of the human dead.[277]

The *lhiannan shee* are believed to be a sort of succubus, attaching themselves to men and haunting them constantly, whilst remaining invisible to everyone but their victims. They can become an intolerable burden to their chosen partners and the men are frequently desperate to escape them, even emigrating to the other side of the world in an attempt to shake them off. There is also a male *lhiannan shee* who is just as dangerous as the female, carrying

---
276 *Yn Lioar Manninagh*, vol.III, 48; see F. Angwin, *Manx Folk Tales*, 'The Silver Cup' & 'The Time Thief.'
277 Broome, *Fairy Tales*, 25 & 67.

off women forever, but much less is reported about him.[278]

Various lhiannan shee have been known at various locations around the island. They seem to haunt wells and pools in particular. One used to live with a man at Glendown; another was seen once walking up the mountain at Port Erin chapel; another was seen chasing her husband at Surby and others have been identified at Kentraghbridge and Ballahick.[279]

The *lhiannan shee* generally come at night, noiselessly, perhaps in the guise of a man's wife. Close proximity to the *lhiannan* is perilous: if they can breathe your breath or touch you, you are in mortal danger. The best thing, then, can be to flee as soon as you spot one. A man was once in the mountains collecting heather when he saw a beautiful woman clad in golden-yellow silk coming towards him. Knowing what she was, he immediately jumped into his cart, whipped his horse and fled for his life. Turning his head to see if she was following him, the man saw the *shee* woman was standing stock-still in the heather, wringing her hands.[280]

Lhiannan shees tend to make the first advance and to reply to them is very dangerous (although they can be banished with a holy word). One man recalled how he had been walking home:

> "it was a very fine night and... I met a young lady in a yellow silk dress rustling as she passed me by. She had a white parasol in her left hand hanging down by her side, but neither of us spoke; afterwards people were telling me it was a *lhiannan shee*, and if I would have spoken to her, she would have followed me."

Another islander recalled:

---

278 I. H. Leney, *Shadowland in Ellan Vannin,* 147; Gill, *Second Manx Scrapbook,* c.6(2).
279 *Manx Notes & Queries,* 1904, no.94; Gill, *Second Manx Scrapbook,* c.6.
280 Cashen, c.2.

> "They are like women and they chase men. Some man was living in Surby, and his wife was away from home one evening, and he went to meet her at night across the fields. He met a woman and thought it was his wife, and spoke to her, and she followed him for long time afterwards. He got clear of her somehow – but I forget the charm."[281]

If a man does make the error of responding to the *lhiannan shee,* she will then become a constant presence beside him, whilst remaining invisible and inaudible to all others around him.

> "There was a *lhiannan shee,* a *white woman,* over at Struan dy Snail, living with a man and they had children together. They were not seen, though local boys would hear them talk and tell their children to keep quiet and go away. The man would know in an instant if anyone was eavesdropping, because she would know and tell him. She and the children could not be seen."[282]

The human partner will eventually be destroyed in body and soul by his faery lover. A man from Derbyhaven was picked up by a *shee* woman at a dance he came across and he was never able to shake her off after that evening. She would make noise all night when everything was quiet. This same story was reported by Evans Wentz, but with significant additional details: a man called Mickleby was walking home at night when he passed a house at Ballahick that was lit up for a party. Two young women were standing outside, who were very amiable and invited him inside. He didn't recognise anyone there but joined in with the dancing and became very friendly with one of the two women who had greeted him. One version of the story records that he made the mistake of wiping the

---
281 Roeder, *Yn Lioar Manninagh,* vol III, 161; Roeder, *Manx Folktales,* 18.
282 Roeder, *Yn Lioar Manninagh,* vol III, 161.

sweat from his face on part of her dress. This created some physical connection between the man and the faery and thereafter she would appear beside his bed at night. Curiously, the only way of getting rid of her was to throw an unbleached linen sheet over the two: perhaps its pure, fresh state was what was significant. In yet another version of this story, when the dancing was over the fairy woman followed Mickleby home and plagued him ever afterward. He went abroad, hoping to leave her behind, but she followed him wherever he went – over sea and land. It was widely supposed he must have kissed her, and it was that contact that gave her the power to haunt him, and to go across the ocean with him.[283]

The *lhiannan shee* can be damaging not only for the male victim, but for his relatives and community, who are neglected and then abandoned. Men would separate themselves from their family and friends to be with these fae lovers, who would visit them nightly and slowly exhaust them – both physically and mentally. In one notorious case a beautiful fairy woman was said to have bewitched all the males of the island and to have lured every one of them into the sea (alternatively, she led them across a wide river, and what appeared to be a shallow ford that could be passed over nearly dry shod turned into a deep and raging torrent that washed the men away). The woman then took the guise of a wren so as to hide from the remaining islanders' vengeance. She escaped, but a spell was placed upon her, requiring her to take the form of a wren every New Year's Day, when she faces being hunted again.[284]

The *lhiannan shee* can involve their partners in their glamour, hiding their movements in sudden fogs and making them both

---

[283] Roeder, *Max Folk Tales,* 1913, 18; Herbert, *Isle of Man,* 1909, 171; Gill, *Second Manx Scrapbook,* c.6; Evans-Wentz, *Fairy Faith,* 124; I. H. Leney, *Shadowland in Ellan Vannin*; *Manx Notes & Queries,* 1904, note 128.

[284] Leney, *Shadowland in Ellan Vannin,* 1890; *Bye Gones,* June 5th 1889, 137; Douglas, *Forgotten Dances,* 9–10; Gill, *Second Manx Scrapbook,* c.9.

vanish, but their long-term influence upon the men is always malign, causing them to waste away and to lose both their wits and human company. For example, a large burly man took up with a fairy woman. He started to share all his food and drink with her, often putting his cup behind him so that she could drink (even though no-one else saw her). As time passed, he began to laugh and talk to himself when alone (or so it seemed to others). He also became paranoid about people trying to listen in to his conversations with her – although he claimed that the *shee* girl was telling him when he was being spied upon.[285]

Manx folklorist Dora Broome described the vampire-like nature of one such *lhiannan shee*. She initially wooed her chosen man by leaving him a chest full of gold and a length of mermaid's hair, but she also hung around his home, sighing and trying to catch his eye, which the man knew could be fateful for him. He decided to get married to a local girl, thinking that this would put the *shee* woman off, but the plan didn't work. The fairy woman continued to hang around, disturbing the newlywed couple, until the husband eventually caught sight of the fairy's lovely face looking through the window. She was "more beautiful than moonlight on water or the first primrose in Spring." The husband fell under her spell instantly and abandoned his wife for seven years. When he finally returned, his erstwhile spouse had remarried and her first husband had been reduced to a white haired, haggard wreck – and could never escape his fairy pursuer. Broome noted that Manx people would say that it is better to jump off a cliff and be drowned than to fall for a *shee* woman, for then there's no peace for the man, who will be cursed to a life of perpetual wandering.[286]

---

285 *Folklore* vol.13, 1902, 'Collectanea' III.
286 Broome, *Fairy Tales*, c.7.

Broome also told us that effective charms against a *lhiannan shee* are to say the Lord's prayer quickly if you glimpse her and to always carry with you a charm, such as twig of *cuirn* (rowan or mountain ash) or the fish bone called a *bollan*. Both are highly effective at repelling fairy lovers, apparently. Powerful protection is needed, though, because "the face of the Fairy Woman is lovelier than a dream and lonelier than a sea-bird's cry."[287] Here's an example of just such a charm working:

> "A man named Maddrell, was walking home late at night. At Kentraugh Bridge a young girl walked up alongside him and he wondered what would she be there for at such an hour. He wondered if she'd got lost and asked her, but she only looked up in his face; but gave him no reply, and he asked her many questions, but no word from her. When they got to Ballacreggan, he turned down the road towards Port St. Mary, and she came that way, too, so he thought she must be a *lhiannan shee*. He spoke to her again, saying: 'If you don't tell me what you are, I'll make a sacrifice of you, by God,' and she grinned in his face and was gone like a flash of lightning."[288]

This next account gives a vivid impression of the nature of a *lhiannan shee* haunting:

> "Harry Ballahane of Rushen Parish was haunted by a lhiannan shee. He was heir to a good farm, but he did very little work on it. Instead, he slept in the barn, and young people used to go to the door to listen because they would hear him talking to someone, but heard only one voice. 'Put it in a *meddyr*' (a small tub), Harry said. Then he muttered, 'Listening, are they? I will give them something else,' and the boys had to run

---

287 Broome, *Fairy Tales from the Isle of Man*, 36–39.
288 Roeder, in *Yn Lioar Manninagh*, vol III, 161.

away as fast as they could. There was a great deal of talk one night, and someone asked Harry next morning what had been happening: 'Yonder dirty thing was in labour,' he said. Harry had been a very good seaman before the *lhiannan* came to him. He'd had an elder brother, and the *lhiannan* had haunted him, until he died. After that, she haunted Harry instead.

Harry always shared his meals with his *shee* woman. He once went out herring-fishing with some other men, and they left him on deck to keep watch. One of the men heard him talking, and he said: 'Will you leave me alone here – what do you want, is it a herring you want?' and he took a herring in his hand and offered it to her, but the man who was looking on, and listening, could not see nor hear her. Harry was sitting alone in the cabin next morning, and when one of the crew came down, he told her to 'shift and make room for the man to sit down.' The man that was to be heir to the farm got married when very young, in dread that Harry would die and the *lhiannan shee* would then come and haunt him; but it seems that she didn't want a third husband, for she must have been old when Harry died."[289]

It's interesting to see the terms in which Harry described his lover: a "dirty thing;" he loathes her, yet he can't escape her.

The *shee* woman might act as a supernatural wife to a man, but she might also compete with the mortal wife – whatever Harry's heir had hoped, and much as the young couple found in Dora Broome's account:

"One followed Nick Kermode's grandfather, when he was a young man, from the fields right into the house. It was dark outside, and he thought she was Shen Moll, his wife, though

---

289 Roeder, *Yn Lioar Manninagh*, vol III, 161; Roeder, *Manx Folktales*, 16.

he was puzzled when she didn't answer him. But when he got in his wife was already there. She couldn't see the fairy woman, and wondered why he wasn't eating his supper. " Don't you see this one? " was his explanation. At that the *shee* grinned at him shockingly and went out through the door."[290]

As we saw a little earlier, on Man *lhiannan shee* women are often called 'White Ladies.' Sometimes they are seen walking with men in classic fairy lover style. For example, in 1898 a man was seen with a White Woman walking at his side from Cregneash up Mull Hill one night, when he claimed he was going onto the hilltop to "take the stars." More often, the *lhiannan shee* as white woman seems to be more or less a ghost, as the next examples show.

Two men were walking past Kirk Arbory one night, and they saw the figure of a woman dressed all in white standing in the angle of the wall just opposite the church gate. When one of the men went to speak to her, she took him by the arm and spun him round until he was dizzy, then let go of him so suddenly that he nearly fell down on the road. The imprint of her fingers remained on his arm up to the day of his death. A very similar incident occurred at Kirk Christ, Rushen. In that case, the apparition was standing just outside the vicarage front-door. The two men thought at first it was the vicar's wife but the figure gripped the man who accosted her, and he had a hard job to get free. He looked years older afterwards, and always had her finger-marks on his arm.[291]

The White Lady of Lewaigue was often seen on Lewaigue Bridge. One time she went right into the nearby farmhouse itself and walked upstairs, dressed in rustling silk, in front of a woman who was living there. The woman was so frightened that she wouldn't stay in the house any longer. This White Lady is believed to have

---

290 Gill, *Third Manx Scrapbook,* Part 2 c.3.
291 Gill, *Third Manx Scrapbook,* Part 2, c.3.

been the ghost of a wronged woman. She also showed herself to a Mr Harrison when he was farming at Lewaigue. He went out of the house one night to look for a man and a pair of horses that were very late getting back from Ramsey. When he was between the gate and the bridge he heard "a rattling (a rustling) like a silk dress, and someone passed him like a shadow and went into the house." However, when he returned inside, he was told that no stranger had been there.[292]

Finally, the reputation of the *lhiannan shee* should not be regarded as being entirely negative. John Matt Mylechreest told how, after his sister and housekeeper had died and he was feeling lonely and ill himself, a *lhiannan shee* came to his door, dressed in shining yellow silk and surrounded by light. She stood and sang to him in an old tongue, until he fell into a healing sleep and woke the next morning wholly cured.[293]

---

292 Gill, *Third Manx Scrapbook*, Part 2 c.3.
293 Mona Douglas, *Restoring to Use our Forgotten Folk Dances*, 2004, 57-58.

Manx Fairies Today

Back at the close of the eighteenth century, it was said that Man was "now about the only place where there is any probability of seeing a fairy." People remained devout believers, especially in the more mountainous districts. A century later, in 1874, the people were still said to be "exceedingly credulous," believing implicitly in fairies and other spirits.[294]

By late Victorian times, though, an interest in fairies was increasingly dismissed as only acceptable in infants, and then only for entertainment, as in a verse published in the *Isle of Man Times* demonstrates:

> "Again a child, he listened with delight,
> To tales of Fairy, Glastin, Buggane and Sprite."

Such material was suitable for scary ghost stories, evidently, but was not viewed more seriously more than that.[295]

As we've seen earlier in the book, some people have blamed the encroachment and noise of industry for scaring the fairies off. Others blamed the hustle and bustle of the tourist trade or the provision

---

294 D. Robertson, *A Tour Through the Isle of Man*, 1794, 75; see too Train, *Isle of Man*, vol.2, c.XVIII and Wood, *History of the Isle of man*, 1811, 159; Jenkinson, *Practical Guide*, 36.
295 *Isle of Man Times*, June 5th 1872, 3 'The Isle-iad.'

of state education, which made older adherents of the fairy faith wary of the risk of "ridicule and scepticism" from younger people. One witness in 1910 felt that schooling was stopping people seeing fairies any longer, but that they were still there "as thick on the Isle of Man as ever they were. They throng the air and darken heaven and rule this lower world."[296]

Yet others have said that fairies are seen less often on the island than they were because people have become sinful and impudent and the fairies no longer wish to make our close acquaintance. Conversely, one Wesleyan minister apparently alleged that the fairies had sailed off to Jamaica in rum barrels – we may presume that they did this to escape his and others' preaching of the gospel and – fortuitously – they took the demon drink with them. An aversion to the gospel was certainly suggested by another writer, who said that the Primitive Methodist chapel at Glen Drink had repelled the local fairies. Others again ascribe the fairies' apparent absence to the fact that they are not made welcome any longer and have become shy and retiring. Also, with few people speaking Manx any longer, they cannot make themselves understood so easily.[297]

Unquestionably, the fairies are preserved for the purposes of attracting tourism (even if, as we have seen, that risks driving them further away). The Fairy Bridge between Ballasalla and Santon is widely promoted as an attraction. Visitors are likewise invited to stop their car facing uphill on the slopes of South Barrule, the fairy mountain, and to release their handbrakes. Their faery faith will be rewarded with the experience of rolling forward up the slope.[298]

Despite all the popularisation and the dire predictions, though, people continue to see the real *ferrishyn*. When Walter Gill was

---

[296] Jenkinson, *Practical Guide*, 75; Wentz 123.
[297] *Mannin*, no.5, 1915, 'Creignish Folklore Notes;' Roeder, *Manx Folktales*, 1; Cumming, *Isle of Man*, 30; Jenkinson, *Practical Guide*, 106.
[298] John Chartres, 'It Helps if You Believe in Fairies,' *The Times*, Nov.25th 1970, 4.

assembling his collections of Manx folklore in the 1920s and '30s, he was by no means dealing with a subject that was dead and consigned to the past. He met people who had seen the little people within only the past few years. This has continued into the present day. For example, in 2010 American writer Signe Pike published *Faery Tale – One Woman's Search for Enchantment in a Modern World*. As part of her research, she visited Ireland, Glastonbury in England, Aberfoyle and Findhorn in Scotland and the Isle of Man, where she spent ten days. Whilst on Man, she had her own faery experiences, including photographing a winged green faery at the old Fairy Bridge near Oakhill; she also recorded earlier experiences, such as a green man snapped in Glen Auldyn in 1994. The *ferrishyn* are still very much present, therefore, for those who have the time and inclination to look for them.[299]

---

299 Pike, *Faery Tale*, 145–6 & 188.

Bibliography

Angwin, F., *Manx Folk Tales*, 2015;

Broome, D., *Fairy Tales from the Isle of Man*, 1963; *More Fairy Tales from the Isle of Man*, 1970;

Carus, Z., *The Green Glass Bottle, Folk Tales form the Isle of Man*, 1975;

Cashen, W., *Manx Folklore*, 1912;

Douglas, M., *Restoring to Use our Almost Forgotten Dances – Writings on the Collection and Revival of Manx Folk Dance & Song*. Isle of Man: Chiollagh Books, 2004;

Gill, Walter, *A Manx Scrapbook*, 3 volumes, 1929 & 1932;

Harrison, William. *Mona Miscellany*, 1869;

Herbert, Agnes. *The Isle of Man*, 1909;

Jenkinson, Henry. *A Practical Guide to the Isle of Man*, 1874;

Killip, M., *Folklore of the Isle of Man*, 1975;

Moore, Arthur. *Folklore of the Isle of Man*, 1891;

Morrison, Sophia. *Manx Fairy Tales*, 1911; 'Dooiney-oie,' *Folklore* vol.23 (1912) 342; 'The buggane ny hushtey – a Manx folktale,' *Folklore*, vol.34 (1923), 349; 'Manx Dialect Connected with Fairies,' *Proceedings of the Isle of Man Natural History and Archaeological Society*, New Series vol.1, 1906;

Penrice, H., *Fables, Fantasies & Folklore of the Isle of Man*, 1996;

Rhys, John. *Manx Folklore and Superstition*. Isle of Man: Chiollagh Books, 1994;

Roeder, Charles. *Manx Folk Tales*. Isle of Man: Chiollagh Books, 1993;

Train, Joseph. *A Historical and Statistical Account of the Isle of Man*, 1845;

Waldron, George. *A Description of the Isle of Man*, 1731.

Appendix: Manx Fairy Poetry

In my 2019 book, *Victorian Fairy Verse,* I examined the late nineteenth century's fascination for faery, a literary genre which matched the parallel popularity of fairies in painting. Much of the verse written at that time was highly generic, repeating increasingly cliched images of feminine little faes with wings and wands. Despite this, Irish and Scottish faery verse was often much more authentic to those countries' folklore, in large measure because it was being used as an assertion of national or even 'Celtic' identity. The Manx verse that follows is part of the same movement; it preserves and celebrates a distinctive island language, culture and mythology.

William Harrison, Y Phynnodderee

This poem was published in the *Isle of Man Times* on Saturday, November 3rd 1883. It is dated October 22nd of the same year and initialled 'W.H.' I assume this to be William Harrison, author of the *Mona Miscellany,* which has been used as a source for this book. Harrison was born in Salford in December 1802, the son of a merchant, and in his youth was involved in a merchant shipping business in Manchester. He retired in 1842 and moved to live on Man. There he served as a member of the House of Keys and as a magistrate. More significantly, he was a founder council member of The Manx Society, editing fifteen of the thirty-one volumes it published. These included three volumes of *Miscellanies*. He was celebrated as a "zealous and painstaking antiquarian [who] will be remembered as having rescued many of our insular ballads, customs, superstitions, and legendary lore from an undeserved oblivion." Harrison died at German on 22nd November 1884, aged eighty-two.

Y Phynnodderee

Dear classic Pan, and art thou gone,
To thy lost Arcady?
Or hearst thou rather when we call
Phynnodderee, Phynnodderee?

Once highest of our fairy court
In sea-girt Mona, thee,
Transformed, we loved our guardian god,
Phynnodderee, Phynnodderee.

Oft seen beneath the moon's pale light,
Amid the elfin glee,
On some weird hill, or glen's green sward,
Phynnodderee, Phynnodderee.

Thou ledst the fairy revel, first
In fairy chivalry,
Ere thou didst love a mortal maid,

Phynnodderee, Phynnodderee.

By malice of thy peers expelled
The elfin coterie,
For thy lost love thou lovedst us,
Phynnodderee, Phynnodderee.

Through wave-lapped Mona, hear no more
Thy plaintive wail shall we,
No more in sweet Glenaldyn now.
Phynnodderee, Phynnodderee.

Borne on the pulses of the breeze,
In fitful melody,
We catch no more thy sad, sweet strain,
Phynnodderee, Phynnodderee.

Thy scanty meed, our choicest sheaf,
In vain we leave for thee,
Or milk bowl touched by maiden lip,
Phynnodderee, Phynnodderee.

The grateful cotter wakes not now
In canny stook to see
His clean-shorn field, or meadow swathed,
Phynnodderee, Phynnodderee.

By toiling fisher, blessed no more
Thy wonted boon shall be-
His ravaged net o'ernight repaired,
Phynnodderee, Phynnodderee.

His barren boat he drags to shore,
Aweary of the sea,

Thou fill'st no more his meshes now,
Phynnodderee, Phynnodderee.

Where youth and maid, together met
Beneath the trysting tree,
The rustling fern betrayed thy watch,
Phynnodderee, Phynnodderee.

Thy tender spirit then would blend
With past sweet memory-
When thou didst love Glenaldyn's maid,
Phynnodderee, Phynnodderee.

No venomed glance of envy marred
Their truthful sympathy;
'Twas thine to fan the kindly flame,
Phynnodderee, Phynnodderee.

To melting youth or musing maid,
By mountain, glen or lea,
Thy liquid music floats no more,
Phynnodderee, Phynnodderee.

Now blight and blank through field and fold,
By hill and dell shall be,
The wind shall thresh our unreaped corn,
Phynnodderee, Phynnodderee.

The ruthless rampage of the gale
Shall work its havoc free,
Now thou art gone, our last best one,
Phynnodderee, Phynnodderee.

On Snaefell bleak or coned Barrule,

Our flocks no more shall flee:
The brewing storm, safe bielded now,
Phynnodderee, Phynnodderee.

Unhouselled shall our younglings die,
The fish desert our sea.
The murrain stalk our midnight shores,
Phynnodderee, Phynnodderee.

Fierce on that metal monster's track
My malison shall be
That dared invade thy peaceful haunts,
Phynnodderee, Phynnodderee.

Upon that snorting dragon fall
My curse right heavily,
That scares thee from thy loved abode,
Phynnodderee, Phynnodderee.

Since last was heard thy parting wail
Far sinking o'er the sea,
Ah – whither shall our prayer pursue
Phynnodderee, Phynnodderee?

Return our gentle Pan, return;
Return good Pan, my chree – *
Or, dearer in our island tongue,
Phynnodderee, Phynnodderee.

cree/ chree – means 'heart.'

Harrison's verse is not great poetry, but it deftly combines several themes of the *fynoderee* folklore: the creature's banishment from fairy for loving a human; his flight from the encroachment of modern civilisation, and his intimate connection to the continued fertility and prosperity of the island – and its decline after his departure.

At the same timer, Harrison cleverly weaves into this a classical comparison to the great god Pan, making the *fynoderee* a musician and protector of true lovers as well as guardian of the flocks and fields of the island.

Cushag: Margaret Letitia Josephine Kermode

What follows is a selection of faery-themed verses taken from the 1907 collection *Poems by Cushag*. Josephine Kermode (1852–1937) was born in Ramsey. Her father was a church minister and, more significantly, president of the Isle of Man Natural History and Antiquarian Society. She had a life-long interest in Manx history and culture and was a close friend of folklorist Sophia Morrison. Writing under the pseudonym, Cushag, Kermode published several plays, stories and volumes of poetry.

As readers will see, Kermode's poems make use of many of the central stories and themes of Manx fairylore. Some of the verse is written in local dialect and it is tied very closely to the landscape and places of the island, emphasising how intertwined the faeries are with the terrain and people of Man. Several of Kermode's other poems mention fairies and fairyland, such as *The Glen of the Twilight, The Tune of His Heart, To the Cushag's Friend, The Dreem Lang* and *The Pool of Ballaquane*, without the little folk being their central subjects. The latter poem is an intriguing one, as it concerns a murdered lover whose ghost returns to take his sweetheart away with him to fairyland; it evokes the *glashtyn* as fatal seducer, without clearly mentioning the beast.

Guillyn Veggey: "The Lil Fallas"

I heard the Guillyn Veggey at the break of day.
On a merry, merry morning in the month of May.
They were hammering an' clamouring an' making such a din-
An' yet there's fallas doubtin' that the like is in!
Clink-a-link, link-a-link, link, link, lin,
Clink-a-link, link-a-link, the hammers ring;
Clink-a-link, link-a-link, ding, ding, ding-
An' yet there's fallas doubtin' that the like is in!

They were hammering their barrels in the cooper's cave,
Sending out the chips to meet the brimming wave.
Working in the hollows of the Cushlin hill,
Turning out their dandy boats an' tackle still.
Clink-a-link, etc.

I heard them in the cave behind the waterfall,
Merry voices echoed by the rocky wall;
While the bay was covered by the chips that flew.
And every chip became a boat with all its crew.
Clink-a-link, etc.

 Oh, lucky is the morning in the month of May,
When you hear the Guillyn Veggey at the break of day,
Hammering an' clamouring an' making such a din-
For they know the herrin's coming, an' there's plenty in!
Clink-a-link, link-a-link, link, link, lin,
Clink-a-link, link-a-link, the hammers ring;
Clink-a-link, link-a-link, ding, ding, ding,
They know the herrin's coming, an' there's plenty in.

MANX FAERIES

The Phynodderee

Ho! Ho! the Phynodderee!
Swinging by himself in the Tramman Tree.
I once was lord of a fairy clan,
But I loved a lass in the Isle of Man;
Her eyes were like the shallows of the mountain stream,
Her hair was like the cornfield's golden gleam
Her voice was like the ringdove's, soft and slow,
Her smile was like the sunbeam's – come and go;
But alas and alack-a-day!
The jealous fairy maids stole my love away.
And now I'm all alone in the Tramman Tree.
Swinging by myself in the Tramman Tree.
Alas and alack-a-day!

Ho! ho! the Phynodderee!
Swinging by himself in the Tramman Tree.
I was once a prince in the fairy land,
But I failed to come at the king's command;
His wrath was like the thunder in the mountain gills,
His eyes were like the lightning on the lone dark hills;
His voice was like the raging of the boiling tide,
As he hurled me down to the earth to bide,
And alas and alack-a-day!
The whole night long I must work away
Till daylight sends me up to the Tramman Tree,
Swinging by myself in the Tramman Tree.
Alas and alack-a-day

Ho! ho! the Phynodderee!
Swinging by himself in the Tramman Tree.

I fetched the stone to Tholt-y-Will;
I saved the sheep on the snow-clad hill;
I saw the storm was coming while the farmer snored;
I drove the sheep before me while the Howlaa roared,
I folded them in safety beneath the creg,
And hunted over Snaefell for the *loaghtan beg*;*
But alas and alack-a-day.
A witch she was, and she would not stay
Till daylight sent me up to the Tramman Tree,
To swing by myself in the Tramman Tree.
Alas and alack-a-day!

Ho! ho! the Phynodderee!
Swinging by himself in the Tramman Tree.
I threshed the corn in the lonely night,
And swept the house in the still moonlight.
I watched the sleeping haggart while the dog took rest,
And drove away the witches that dared molest;
I milked the cows at dawning and eased their heads,
And soothed the patient horses in their tired beds,
But alas and alack-a-day!
The farmer thought I worked because I wanted pay!
And left a coat and breeches for the poor Phynodderee;
So his lassie cannot see him in the Tramman Tree
Swinging by himself in the Tramman Tree.
Alas and alack-a-day.

* *loaghtan beg* – this is the native brown Manx sheep.

The Passing of The Fayries

"An' was there a dhrop between us?"
That's what they're sayin' still.
An' never a dhrop was there at all,
But a crowd of wans in the road for all,
An' sthrivin' up the hill.

The dawn was barely sthreakin'
An' a sup o' rain doin' in;
But liftin' as the day grew on,
Like dhryin' up when the night was gone,
With a scutch o' risin' win'.

An' here was these wans comin',
An' creepenin' up the side,
With a surt of murmerin', wailin' soun'
That seemed to be risin' all aroun',
Like the soun' of the weary tide

There was oul', an' young, an' childher,
All bended under loads;
With beds an' crocks, an' spuds, an' grips,
An' spinnin' wheels, an' taller dips,
All filin' up the roads.

From Earey Beg an' Earey Moar,
Over the broken bridge;
Over the pairk at Earey Glass,
By Balla'himmin and up Rhenass,
An' all along the ridge.

An' toilin' up Bearey Mountain,
With that wailin', sighin' soun'
As if their hearts were goin' a-breakin',
The for their last leave they were takin',
Wherever they were boun.'

An' Bearey was roulin' his cloak,
An' reachin' it down his side,
An' coaxin' them up an' lappin' them roun',
Till the wailin' was dyin' gradjual down,
Like the calm of the ebbing tide.

MANX FAERIES

The Ride

It happened once upon a time
I met the Fairies straying,
From under Bearey's Cap they came
To go once more a-Maying.

They came about me in the mist,
I heard their songs and laughter,
And some went dancing on before
And some came singing after.

My nag was shod with fairy shoes
And bred among the mountains,
And many a moonlight prank she played
Along the streams and fountains.

We scampered down by Greeba Mills
And on to old St. Trinian's,
And hastened lest the Big Buggane
Should join us on his pinions.

Though steep as Ugh ta breesh ma chree
The road to green Ballinghan,
My nag stepped out with might and main—
Her like is not in Englan'.

For up she went and on she went
Above the trees o'erarching,
And on the Braid we turned to see
The mountains all come marching.

From Greeba Towers to Laxey Glen
Their noble heads up-lifting,
And far behind them in the blue
Their fleecy helmets drifting.

St. Mark's and Sluggadhoo we passed
And came to Ballamoddha,
And here my Fairy Company
Fell into some disorder.

For men, they said, and motor-cars
Have spoiled the roads for Fairies,
We'll meet you further on, they said,
Among the lonely Gareys.

I scarce had gone a mile before
My steed began to blether,
Her fairy shoes, she said, were best
For travelling through the heather.

So round she went, and West she went,
And through the pleasant Gareys,
And here I met my friends again,
My company of Fairies.

And over Colby Bridge we raced
And through the Croit-y-Caley,
And all the folk from Cronk-Howe-Moar
Came out to meet us gaily.

Then up Cregneash we went like storm
For day began to hurry,
And at the circle met the sun
And stayed at Lag-ny-Wurry.

And on the Hill we danced till eve
And round about the hollow,
Till all the bones got up and joined
And set themselves to follow.

"No, no," we said, "not so," we said,
"Our ways are not together;
We'll take the road and go," we said
"Stay you and watch the weather."

My nag was fed by fairy hands,
She drank from Chibbyr-Garvel
And in a trice, she leapt aloft
And left the bones to marvel.

The mist came floating round again
With songs and laughter ringing-
And there we were on Bearey slopes
Where morning larks were singing.

(from) The Babe of Earey Cushlin

From Niarbyl Point to Bradda Head
The great Bay Mooar lies broad and deep,
And here the fishers cast their nets,
While landward folk are lost in sleep.

With steady sweep of heavy oars,
From Dalby strand they make their way,
Before the lingering light has left
The crags of Cronk-ny-Iree Lhaa.

Sometimes the night is loud with storm,
Sometimes the creeping fog comes round,
And sometimes all the moonlit hours
Are holy with a peace profound.

Sometimes between the dusk and dark
The fishers see a glancing spark,
A tiny riding-light;
Now here– now there–
And now a pair,
And now a score,
And everywhere
Around them dancing bright.
And straightway all about them ride
The fairy nickeys on the tide;
And all the air is full of din,
And elfish voices, shrewd and thin,
And creak of spar,
And smell of tar,
And water washing up the side;

MANX FAERIES

While here and there,
And everywhere,
The gentle folk
Are well bespoke,
And room is left for them to ride
In safety on the gleaming tide.
And then a puff
Of wind comes by,
"Oie-vie, oie-vie!" the fairies cry.
And all around the sea is bare,
And not a boat is anywhere!

And that's the time the men would find
Good luck with all the nets they cast,
And rowing slow with loaded store,
Be home before the night was past.

But other times the fish was scarce,
And some would stay and some would go,
About the Sloc or further out
Or back to sleeping Dalby, row.

And sometimes only one alone
Would drift along the shadowy land,
And in the darkness quake to hear
The Babe at Earey-Cushlin strand.

Two mates were drifting thus one night
In lonely silence on the Bay,
Such silence as old comrades know
That means more than a man can say.

Then spoke at last the younger man–
"The Babe is fretting sore to-night;
And pitiful it is to hear
Its cries up yonder on the height!"

And then the twain began to speak
Of that sad story of the place;
And question why such things should he
And what could limit Saving Grace.

"For seemeth me," the elder said,
"That babe hath more than common loss,
For it was born on holy ground
Though never named with sign of cross."

"And seemeth me," he musing said,
"It must have been so nearly saved,
That even now it might be blest
If any man the deed had braved."

"And surely God's own heart must ache
To hear it sobbing through the dark,
And long to have its christened soul
Beside Him in the sheltering ark."

"Your tender babes are safe at home,
And cradled in their mother's prayers;
My sturdy sons to manhood grown,
Have long repaid my early cares."

"The very hawks upon the hill
Watch their fierce brood through calm and storm;
And timid conies in the fern
Keep their soft younglings safe and warm."

"And will not He who made them all
Watch o'er His little lost ones too,
And, maybe waited till this hour,
For us poor men His Will to do."

And then the other made reply–
"Let us christen the Babe if that be so,
And if we are doing the Will of the Lord
He will send us a token, that we shall know."

And these men of the sea stood up in the boat,
That under them gave, and rocked, and swayed,
And their hearts o'erflowed with a mighty faith,
And they spake with God and were not afraid.

And they signed the Cross on the midnight air,
While the lifting billows rolled and fell,
And the star of night was their altar-light,
And the deep sea sounded their vesper bell.

And the elder lifted his sea-worn hand,
And bared to the sky his rev'rent head;
While the younger followed him word by word.
And thus to the Babe they spoke and said–

"If thou'rt a boy thy name shall be Juan,
If thou'rt a girl thy name shall be Joan."
And the crying ceased and the Babe was still
And the sound of the sea was heard alone.

And a star shot up from the lone dark Keeill*
And a soul flew free from the throes of night;
And their eyes were opened that they could see
The Babe's glad welcome to fields of light.

And they heard the music of harps on high
While the lifting billows rolled and fell,
Till the sun rose over the watching Cronk
And the deep sea sounded their matin bell.

* A *keeill* is an ancient chapel.

MANX FAERIES

The Wans From Up

"Mother," she said, "when you're not by,
There's lil wans talkin' to me,
They're showin' me pictures out in the sky,
Where the sun sets over the sea.
Will I lave a piece of my supper," she said,
"An' a dhrop of milk in the cup?
D'you think its Fayries thass in?" she said.
 – I'm thinkin' 'twas Wans from Up.
"Mother," she said, "when the nights is long
There's lil wans comin' to me.
They're bringin' a harp an' makin' a song,
And houlin' a light to see.
I'll lave a bit of my supper," she said,
"An' a tase of milk in the cup;
I'm thinkin' it's Fayries thass in," she said.
 – But I knew it was Wans from Up.
Mother," she said, "my head is sore,
An' the lil wans is callin' me;
They say there's a boat waitin' down at the shore
To take me a sail on the sea.
Keep by a piece of my supper," she said,
"An' lave some milk in the cup;
I'll go with the Fayries a bit," she said.
 – An' she went to the Wans from Up.

(I assume that 'the ones from up' are actually meant to be angels, who take the daughter away, but we learn about popular beliefs regarding the little people as a result of her misidentification).

Lightning Source UK Ltd.
Milton Keynes UK
UKHW021005270921
391255UK00005B/180

9 781838 418533